TRUCK STOP

John Penney

Encyclopocalypse Publications
www.encyclopocalypse.com

Contents

One

A cold, eerie feeling crept over Cindy as she stared at the old bulletin board filled with missing-persons notices. The faces on the board could easily have been her friends, her sister, even her mother staring back at her from the yellowing, faded pictures. Some of the faces had been missing since the early '90s, others more recently. One of the pretty young girls, wearing braces, with freckles and sandy blonde hair, had been reported missing just eight months ago.

Cindy took a shallow, unsteady breath and looked up and down the dark, empty hallway. She had stopped unwillingly at this strange place in the Utah mountains, more an abandoned building than the promised diner and gift shop. She had come back here to use the bathroom and had become distracted by this strange, shrine-like bulletin board. A faint buzzing sound echoed from a fluorescent bulb that flickered back down the empty hall she had traversed, where a sign pointed to showers and sleeping rooms. Cindy couldn't imagine anyone wanting to spend the night here. The commercial-grade burnt orange carpet was stained and dirty, and there were dark black streaks at the doorway entrances from years of foot traffic. The walls were a dingy yellow.

Cindy knew she should continue to the bathroom, but when she glanced back at the bulletin board, she was transfixed again. She couldn't help feeling that there was something terrifying about this place.

She had felt this way before, but she had learned her lesson about saying anything when she tried to tell her boyfriend at the time. He had laughed at her and called what she felt "Cindy's ghost stories" when he talked to their friends later. After that, when they were alone together and he saw that he had hurt her feelings, he tried to make her feel better by assuring her that there was nothing to be afraid of; if there were ghosts, they couldn't touch her from beyond the grave.

But this feeling was different. It was as if these people were near her; their faces were trying to warn her of something dark, evil, and very much a part of her world. Something that was close to her at that moment.

Cindy felt another shiver go down her spine. She checked her watch. It was ten p.m. now; she would be able to get to Salt Lake City if she pushed on tonight. She hadn't originally planned on driving alone, but her roommate, who had been going to spend Christmas with her, had decided at the last moment to go to Hawaii instead.

Cindy had been angry, of course, but she had smiled the way she usually did in situations like that. She always went along to get along; Cindy's cousin used to tell her it was because she was the daughter of divorce. She was always desperately wanting to make peace between her ever-warring parents.

Cindy was a junior at the University of Las Vegas. Her mother hadn't been thrilled about Cindy leaving Salt Lake City to go to school, but Cindy had fought it. She got her own loans and was doing it herself. Now, she was driving home alone to see her mother. In only another three hours she would be there, warm and safe again for the holidays.

Cindy pulled her eyes off the disturbing bulletin board and turned to leave. That's when she felt the stinging cold slap of a rubber-gloved hand on her mouth and the blinding pain, as something dull and heavy slammed into the back of her head.

Then there was blackness.

There would be no scream from Cindy to alert anyone.

Seconds, minutes, hours. Even days could have gone by. There was no way to tell.

A burning, acrid smell filled Cindy's nostrils. She heard a distant metallic grinding sound. An electric hum. Her mouth hurt at the edges where it was stretched wide. There was something spongy and cloth-like reaching deep down her throat.

She tried to force her eyes open, but her lids managed to open to only a thin crack. Her vision was blurry and smeared; shapes were drifting strangely past her so that she couldn't focus. What she could see was dim, yellow, and blotchy. The grinding stopped, and the electric hum faded away.

She heard her own breathing and the faint thump of her heart in her ears. Then footsteps approached. She strained her vocal cords to speak, but she couldn't make it happen. The cloth choked back any sound.

A dull metallic thump resonated through her body, making her vibrate involuntarily. She was confused, and she panicked. Then an excruciating pain shot up her shoulder. Another thump, and her other arm burned horribly.

Deep in the basement of her mind, she knew what was happening to her. She was being dismembered. The feeling where her arms had been was distant and throbbing. Next, there was a ragged burning sensation at her ankles as her feet were separated from her legs. Finally, she felt a warm rush surge over her body as she bled out.

Then blackness again. Silence. Permanence.

She was with them now. The ones who had tried to warn her.

* * *

Cedar Mountain Truck Stop was a sprawling, run-down compound at the foot of an isolated mountain pass in Utah. Muddy big rigs rumbled in and out of the large parking lot. It had been state of the art thirty years ago. Now, it was a shell of its former self.

In the main building, which was fronted by a bay of gas pumps, there was a twenty-four hour diner with a gift shop attached. Most of the time there was no one at the register in the gift shop. If you wanted to buy any of the travel aids that gathered dust on the dingy glass shelves, you had to get the waitress's attention, or better yet, just bring what you wanted to the diner. Mostly the gift shop sold Tylenol, condoms, and any number of stay-awake products. Beyond the gift shop was the long hallway that led to the sleeping rooms, showers, and bathrooms for long-haul truckers. There was a huge, cavernous truck wash, and a similarly oversized building for truck repairs away from the main building.

No one knew it, but Cedar Mountain was more than just a routine stop for truckers. It was the place where people went missing.

It was a typical weekday night. There were a lot of big rigs in the parking lot and only a couple of civilian cars. No one paid any notice to the lone figure straining with the weight of two heavy plastic garbage bags as it went behind the main building, past the large truck wash, then beyond the repair garage. The figure ducked through a hole in the cyclone fence that led to a junkyard filled with old truck parts, discarded appliances, and old mattresses.

It was not surprising that no one paid any particular attention to the shadowy figure, or to anyone else moving around on the property, for that matter. This was the way it always was at Cedar Mountain. Transitory. Anonymous. It was the perfect place for a predator to hunt prey.

And Cindy had just been the latest in a long line.

Two

It was a cold night, even for the Nevada desert in December. The black clouds that hung over the aging tract home development on the outskirts of Las Vegas had come down from the north, heavy with impending rain.

Roger Dalton pulled his '74 Mustang to a stop in front of the dilapidated sign on the brown lawn of the Palm Ridge Estates. It was an exotic name for a man-made oasis of cheaply built townhouses dating from the early '80s.

Roger shut off the engine and twisted the rear-view mirror so that he could get a good look at his reflection. His heavy black eyeliner was smeared beneath his left eye. No doubt, he had rubbed it at some point. He hoped he had done so some time after he had finished playing the last set at Stateline three hours earlier. He hated the pretentiousness of using makeup and did it only because the rest of the band members wore it too.

Roger dug around on the seat next to him, found an unused napkin in a McDonald's bag, and spit on it. He wiped his eyes hard, and most of the eyeliner came off, enough so that it was barely noticeable in the darkness. Roger performed a final survey of his face; it was still handsome in that slightly gaunt, emo way. His shaggy black hair was his calculated effort to remain young looking.

In Roger's business, closing in on 30 was like hitting retirement. Especially the way his career had gone. He had made it big enough to keep in the game, but never big enough to make any real "fuck you" money. He was a workaday rhythm guitarist.

Most people would have given their right nut to make a living as a musician. But Roger was over that. He was tired. Making that living had come at a high price, and he had only recently realized it, when he looked back on the train wreck of relationships he had left in his wake. The long stream of groupies looking up at him from their knees never saw who he really was, only what they wanted him to be. And Roger had never been what anyone could have guessed.

Roger was gifted—and he was cursed, cursed in ways he could never tell normal people. He had tortured himself for years trying to drown out the curse, but it was futile. The one thing he wanted most was to be normal, but it was the one thing he could never be.

Roger jumped out of the Mustang, grabbed his guitar off the back seat, stashed it in the trunk, and started up the walkway. He kicked a broken tricycle off the pathway, stepped up to the condo door, and knocked. He waited, glanced around at the graffiti covering the walls of the patios of the other units. There was no answer. He sighed anxiously, knocked louder.

"Zoe! Open up!" Roger rubbed his tired eyes, waited a moment longer. "Shit."

He peered over the low-lying porch wall and through the living room window. The curtain was partially open, and he could see there was a light on inside. He could also hear the muffled sound of a droning TV.

Roger shifted his angle and saw a lamp on the floor near a few broken dishes. Nothing unusual. Not when it came to the way his ex-wife lived.

Roger leaned up close to the crack in the door, cupped his mouth. "Zoe, come on. Look, I know I'm late. Just let me get Lilly, and I'll be out of here."

Still nothing from inside.

"Fuck. Come on, Zoe. Open the fucking door. I want Lilly." Roger clenched his fist and raised it, about to pound again, when a little voice came from behind him.

"Daddy?"

Roger spun around, startled. Lilly, Roger's adorable seven-year-old daughter was standing by the side door of the condo carrying her backpack and her favorite stuffed rabbit. Despite the apparent inattention of her mother, she was ready to go.

Roger hurried over to her. "Oh, sweetie," he said. He scooped the backpack off her little shoulders, kneeled down, and gave her a big hug and a kiss, "Daddy is so sorry he's late."

"You were supposed to be here yesterday," his daughter said with a yawn.

Roger choked back the pang of guilt that shot through his gut. "I know, I know. Your mom didn't tell you that another gig at Stateline came up at the last minute when I was finishing in L.A.?"

The little girl shook her head.

Roger hugged her again, "I'm sorry. But I called her."

Lilly smiled, held up her faded pink stuffed rabbit "It's okay, Daddy. Jimmie Jerry got lonely for you, that's all."

Roger returned the smile. "I know. And I got lonely for Jimmie Jerry too." He gave the old rabbit a kiss and took Lilly's little hand. "Come on."

Roger led her down the walkway as he dialed his cell phone. "Is your mom asleep in there?"

"She's with Jack," Lilly revealed.

Roger hesitated at the sound of Jack's name.

"Jack? Jack came back to visit again?"

"Yeah. He sleeps a lot," the little girl answered.

Roger frowned, annoyed. His ex-wife's voice mail message crackled over the phone. "It's Zoe. You know what to do."

Roger waited impatiently for the tone and jumped in. "Hey, Zoe. I've got Lilly." Roger looked down at his daughter, then lowered his voice and continued. "Listen, I thought we discussed the whole Jack thing. You know how I feel about that motherfu—" Roger caught himself at the last second "—asshole being around when Lilly's there. And you should've told her I wasn't coming until today. It's not—" Roger looked down at Lilly once again. It was clear that the little girl was listening to every word he said, "Look, just…just call me when you get this message."

Roger snapped off the phone, took a deep breath, then smiled. "It's great to see you, honey," he said to Lilly.

The little girl frowned. "Did I get Mommy in trouble again?"

"Of course not," Roger assured her. "The only one who can get Mommy in trouble is Mommy. Come on, we've got a long drive."

He opened the car door for her, and she climbed into the back seat, shoving aside the blanket he had put there for her, knowing she would want to sleep.

Three

Roger's Mustang sped down the dark desert freeway, heading east. Fat raindrops began to splat on the windshield. Roger twisted the knob, and the old wipers groaned as they scraped across the dusty glass, smearing the distant pinpoints of light on the horizon. He shot a glance back at Lilly, who was cuddled up in the back seat with her stuffed rabbit and the blanket. She looked tiny there, her long brown hair slightly mussed and falling over the pink toy, looking tired. Roger remembered her yawn and wondered whether she was getting enough sleep.

She looked up and saw that he was looking at her. "Where's Sea Salt City?" she asked.

"Salt Lake City," he corrected. "And it's in Utah. We won't be there until morning."

"How long are we staying there?"

"Daddy's playing tomorrow night and the night after. Then we come home again."

"Where do I sleep?"

"At your Aunt Cathy's. Remember her?"

Lilly nodded, then dropped her head onto her rabbit and yawned.

Roger smiled. "You'll like it there. They have a nice house. They even have a pool."

The raindrops started coming faster and harder. Roger turned up the wipers, which caused an unnerving grinding sound. The blades were worn almost to the metal.

Roger cursed under his breath. "Shit." The blurry mess began to clear.

They traveled along for a moment in silence, then

he said, "Honey, after this weekend, I'm going to start playing in a bar at home in Las Vegas. I'll only be gone for a few hours a night."

Lilly's little blue eyes looked up at him from her resting position. "With the band?"

Roger took a moment before answering "No, they…they're still going to tour without me."

"What about our record deal?"

It had always been "our" record deal. Roger had made sure of that. He figured if Lilly looked at his career as if it belonged to both of them, she'd understand when he had to go away for so long at a time. It was a self-serving move, of course, and Roger had grown to see it as embarrassing, but the terms of the deal had stuck with Lilly. And now it was going to all backfire if she was that invested in "their" record deal.

"Well, that…that didn't work out," Roger proceeded carefully. Sure enough, a disappointed look started to cloud his daughter's face. Roger added quickly, "But you never know. I might be able to get a deal myself."

Roger's feint didn't do much to change Lilly's reaction. He sighed and decided to take a chance and deal with it head on. "Look, my deal is going to be much better. I won't have to leave you with your mother again. Won't that be good?"

Lilly nodded, yawned again. Her eyes were growing heavy.

Roger watched her for a moment and continued, "Lilly, I'm sorry about tonight. I should have talked to you on the phone myself to tell you I wasn't coming yesterday, but I promise it's not going to happen again. From now on, we're going to be together all the time."

Lilly nodded again. A faint smile crossed her face

as she pulled the blanket around her and drifted off to sleep, her head resting on the pink rabbit.

* * *

The rain was coming down heavily by the time Roger pulled his Mustang off the highway and into the Cedar Mountain Truck Stop. It was getting close to two a.m., and they had been on the road for hours. He squinted through the windshield as the tattered blades ground back and forth in a futile attempt to clear the onslaught of water.

He carefully steered toward the metal canopy that covered the aging gas pumps in front of the diner. His car rolled to a stop underneath, and he shut down the engine. He sighed—finally, a break from the rain.

He glanced into the back seat where Lilly was fast asleep under her blanket. "Just gotta get some gas, honey," he said. He knew she probably couldn't hear him, but it seemed important to tell her. He yanked open the car door.

The gas pump island was a good twenty-five yards in front of the main building. A muscular, bald, mid-40s truck stop mechanic was busy trying to prop up a broken panel in the leaky canopy over the pumps with a mop handle.

Roger gave him a cursory nod as he crossed to the pump and slid his card into the slot. He wiped away the heavy mist over the digital display, leaned down close, and tried to decipher the instructions. Given the age of the rest of the place, he was surprised to see that he could use his card and didn't have to pay the attendant first.

"Fuck cats and dogs, this is raining goddamn buffalos," the mechanic said, smiling sardonically.

Roger glanced over at the man, who was looking over at him now.

"Raining all the way from Nevada?" the mechanic continued.

Roger shrugged. "Not all the way." He jammed the nozzle into his tank and cranked the handle over. Fuel began rushing into his tank. Roger stretched his neck, looked over at his tattered wipers. He considered them for a moment, then crossed to his trunk and popped it open. He shoved aside his guitar case, pushed some dirty clothes out of the way, and found the roll of duct tape he was looking for. He pulled out an old shirt, ripped it in half, and crossed back to the windshield.

The bald man paused again and looked over at Roger as he started wrapping a piece of his old shirt around the wiper arm. "I got plenty of blades in the shop."

Roger tore off a piece of tape and started securing the cloth to the arm. "Thanks, but I'm a little short of funds tonight."

"I take all kinda plastic," the mechanic pressed.

"That's okay. Thanks, anyway." Roger finished securing the pieces of cloth to the wiper arms, then crossed back to the pump.

The man smiled to himself. "Suit yourself, but that ain't gonna hold. Not in weather like this."

Roger ignored the warning, finished at the pump, and opened his car door.

The mechanic shook his head and watched as Roger started up the old Mustang and slowly cruised across the parking lot toward the diner at the front of the main building.

The odd mechanic was right. The soggy, shirt-wrapped wipers flung themselves back and forth across the windshield in a blurry attempt to stem the pouring rain. They worked, but barely. Certainly not good enough if it was going to come down like this all the way to Salt Lake City.

Roger pulled to a stop right outside the large diner window and shut off the engine. He clicked off the headlights and sat for a moment in the car. The sound of rain drummed loudly on the roof.

"Shit." He rubbed his tired eyes, exhausted, then peered out at the aging truck stop complex. The expansive parking lot was fairly quiet, with just the occasional truck coming and going. A young couple had pulled up to the gas pumps. A family—husband, wife, and two kids, sheltered by raincoats held over their heads, were hurrying into the diner from their minivan. The rain was coming down in sheets.

Roger deliberated. He had to be in Salt Lake the next day for the gig, but he was too tired to keep going without coffee or a Red Bull. He hated to wake Lilly, though. He looked back at her, sound asleep, then looked over at the large diner window only a few steps away. If he went inside for a moment to get some coffee, he wouldn't even have to take his eyes off the car.

Roger grabbed his sweatshirt and slipped it on. He pulled the hood over his head and opened the car door. He hopped out, closed the door quietly behind him, carefully locked the doors, and ran into the diner.

Four

Kajagoogoo's "Too Shy" played on the ratty ceiling speakers in the timeworn diner. A real blast from the past, Roger thought as he yanked off his hood and brushed the water off his shoulder.

Lucinda, a sad, sexy-looking twenty-year-old with "affordable hooker" written all over her, looked up from the far end of the counter as Roger approached the register. He avoided her desperate smile and looked back out the big window to his car, which was in plain view just a few yards away.

The night-shift waitress dropped off a patty melt to a heavyset trucker at the counter, then met Roger at the register. She was a rocker in her early 20s with a purple streak in her jet-black hair, a small gold ring piercing her lower lip, and, of course, the requisite black nail polish. "Hey," she said.

Roger glanced at her before looking out the window at the car again. "Hey. How's it going"?

She smiled and nodded at the dingy diner around her. "Really?"

Roger looked back at her, and this time he saw her for the first time. She was cute. He smiled back. "That bad, huh?"

She folded her order pad over to a new page and hesitated. A slow look of recognition crossed her face. "Fuck me," she said. "You're rhythm guitar for Cutt, right?"

Roger was surprised, and a bit flattered. "I am, yeah."

"You guys rocked The Palms last year when you opened for Evanescence."

Roger's smile broadened involuntarily. "Thanks. Thanks a lot. I'm Roger—"

"Dalton. Right, I know." She was beaming now as she finished his words.

"Cool," was all Roger could come up with as he admired the way her smile wrinkled her nose in an adorable way.

She wiped her hand on her apron and thrust it out to him confidently. "Kat. I'm Kat Richards."

Roger took her hand and shook it. They both stood there for a moment without saying anything. It was like two members of the same tribe meeting on foreign shores. Kindred rocker spirits.

Kat snapped out of it first. "So, what can I get you?"

"Just, uh, coffee. Oh no, wait. One of those Five Hour Energy drinks." He pointed to the display by the register.

"Anything else?"

Roger thought a moment. "Yeah. Soup, maybe, to go."

"Yeah? Well we got minestrone and, well, minestrone. The mushroom sucks."

"Done deal."

Roger watched as Kat jotted down the order on her ticket, then turned and jammed it onto the wheel in the pass-through. Cute legs. Rocking body. And that hair. She was more than cute. She was hot.

Kat spun back with a big smile on her face. "So, what are you doing out here?"

Roger's eyes snapped back to her face. "Going to Salt Lake for a gig."

"No shit. I didn't know you guys were going to be playing Salt Lake."

Roger hesitated; he had blurted out where he was

going so she wouldn't notice he had been checking her out. But now he had to explain more than he wanted to. "Yeah, well. It's probably my last time with Cutt."

"Really?"

"Yeah, I'm going to start playing in Vegas full time by myself."

"Oh, nice. Where?"

Shit. No way out of this now, Roger thought. He had only met her five minutes ago, and he was already going to have to let her know what a loser he was. He could probably try to spin it, but in the end, he couldn't hide from it. She would eventually find out, along with the rest of the world. After all, the casino wasn't going to keep the gig a secret. He decided to just offer up the truth and get it over with. "At, uh, Circus Circus. The lounge there in the amusement part."

"You mean where they have that roller coaster?"

Could this have gone worse? The cool rocker dude was going to be playing at a bar in a carnival. Roger could only smile and fess up. "Yeah."

There was a moment that seemed like an eternity to Roger, then Kat nodded and smiled. "I am so there."

What did she say? Roger could barely hide his surprise. "Yeah?"

"Definitely." And he could tell she totally meant it. Another moment lingered between them, then the bell dinged behind her.

The middle-aged cook and night manager pushed the Styrofoam container across the reach-through, "Order up." He grunted, then went back to his grill.

Kat said, "Thanks, Bart," grabbed the soup, and handed it to Roger. He dug out his wallet, pulled out some cash.

"Three fifty. Oh, and one of these Five Hour little

guys here." She handed him one of the small drinks. "These little suckers are two-fifty. Six total."

Roger handed her a ten. She smiled and shook her head as she rang him up. "Roger fucking Dalton. Too cool."

She turned back to him with his change. Roger waved her off. "Yours."

Kat dropped the change in her apron. "Thanks." She laughed. There was another of their now-familiar awkward moments.

Roger jumped in. "So, I'm starting next month. At Circus Circus. I'll look for you."

"You'll see me," she assured him.

"Cool." He grabbed his soup. "Cool," he repeated. He started to turn, then hesitated. He looked out the big front window at his nearby car, then back to Kat, "Hey, uh, y'know, I've got my daughter in my car right there. Any chance you could keep an eye on it? I gotta use the bathroom."

"Right there? The Mustang?"

"Yeah."

She looked back at him, still smiling. "Sure, sure. Of course. No problem."

"Really? Thanks. It's just that it's pouring, and she's asleep. I didn't want to drag her out in this shit, you know."

"I got it," she reassured him.

Roger sighed, relieved. "That's great. Thanks, really. I'll be quick."

"I'll be here."

Roger turned and scanned the diner with a puzzled look on his face.

Kat had seen that look a million times before. "Out that back door," she explained, "past the gift shop, all the way at the end of the hall. Last door on the right."

"Thanks." Roger smiled and started out across the diner; he was careful to avoid Lucinda's hopeful, sad smile as he passed her by.

* * *

The thin, scratchy '80s Muzak took on an eerie quality in the long, dark hallway to the bathroom. Drops of water splashed from several leaks in the stained ceiling into metal pots set on the ancient orange carpet. Roger started toward the bathroom doors in the shadowy distance. On the way, he passed several doors to the showers and several more that were sleeping rooms.

Then he approached it: the old bulletin board, filled with the years of yellowing missing-persons notices, and he couldn't help but stop.

Just as Cindy had.

Roger unscrewed his Five Hour Energy drink and took a sip as he looked over the clutter. There was something about the collage of faces that would not be ignored. It was almost hypnotic. The yellowing fliers rattled slightly as a light cold breeze rippled past them. An uneasy feeling began to creep up on Roger.

But Roger ignored the feeling. He downed the rest of his little drink, pried his eyes away, and continued to the men's room. He pushed open the creaking door.

It was dingy in here too, with rust stains in the cracked sinks. The fluorescent bulbs overhead flickered and buzzed. Roger tossed his empty energy drink bottle away, stepped up to the urinal, unzipped, and exhaled slowly.

He stood for a long moment, relieving himself.

He could hear the wind and the wash of rain outside. There was the dim rumble of an occasional truck approaching and another departing, then there was something else. It was a distant scratching sound.

Roger clamped off in midstream. He remained at the urinal for a moment, waiting. Then it happened again. A scraping sound, like human fingernails on hollow wood. This time, it was followed by a low thump.

Then silence.

Roger closed his eyes and concentrated, and after a moment, he was able to resume his business. He zipped up, crossed back to the sink. He splashed water on his hands and looked around for a towel, but none was to be found. He patted his hands dry on his pants and crossed back to the door.

Roger stepped back out into hallway and paused. He looked down the long, dark corridor. At the far end was a door with a small, high windowpane leading outside. Rain drummed against the glass.

Roger remained there, waiting. A minute passed, and another. Roger took a deep, cleansing breath and started down the hall.

He had only gotten a few steps when lightning flashed outside the glass pane in the door. For a brief second the flickering light silhouetted the figure of a woman standing just inside the door.

Roger stopped cold. Shit. Did he just see that?

He waited for another moment. Thunder rattled the old building. There was no one in front of the door.

Roger pushed himself on down the hall. As he passed the old bulletin board, the eerie Muzak buzzed and distorted. Then, faintly, the vague sound of what seemed like a woman sobbing blended with the song. Roger hesitated, listened more carefully. But it was just the distorted Muzak again. Roger continued.

He reached the exit door with the small window and stopped. Maybe he had just seen a shadow from something outside.

He straightened up as far as he could and peered out the small, high window into the rainy darkness. He couldn't see much. It was dark and blurry. He squinted, reached up, and wiped the condensation off the inside.

It didn't make things much better. Smeared glass must be his destiny tonight. First his windshield wipers and now this.

He sighed and was just about to turn away when there was a loud slap at the window. He spun back, startled. A bloody hand was clawing at the glass, its fingers clutching at the top of the small frame as though to pull itself up.

Roger recoiled, horrified. The hand slowly streaked down the glass, leaving a bloody trail behind.

Roger snapped out of his stunned paralysis. He shoved the door hard, and it banged all the way open.

There was no one there.

Roger leaned outside and scanned the darkness. He saw the junkyard a few yards away. Off to the right was the repair garage, and off to the left was the truck wash. But there was no sign of the woman, or of anyone.

Roger stood for a moment in silence.

Shit. It had happened again. He thought he had tuned it out, but he hadn't.

He had spent his life struggling with this. His encounters. It didn't matter that some people told him it was a blessing. It wasn't. It was a curse. Plain and simple.

Roger couldn't have known anything about Cindy, let alone that she had walked that same corridor that same night. He couldn't have known that they were both sensitives. But Roger was a much stronger sensitive than Cindy. He had seen the other side before. Heard it. Even interacted with it.

Roger's encounters had started when he turned thirteen. Puberty. That awkward phase when his body was in complete turmoil. At first, he tried to pretend they didn't happen, but they only got stronger. Whatever physiological changes his body had undergone at that point in his life turned him on like a human antenna. The changes allowed him to tune into things that others couldn't see or hear.

He had struggled for a while, afraid to say anything to anyone, but he had finally broken down and confided in a free-spirited friend of his older sister's. She didn't bat an eye; she was the first person to tell him that it was a gift.

Roger was relieved at first, and it even got him laid for the first time with her, but when the affair died out, it all backfired. The free spirit told Roger's sister all about his encounters.

There were psychologists. Then psychiatrists. There were concerned counselors from his school, and even an ex-priest friend of the family who weighed in.

Then, finally, there was the diagnosis. Schizophrenia. He went on a few years of heavy medication and, unfortunately, it helped him. It was unfortunate because the drugs also dulled him so much he couldn't play his music.

Roger started taking himself off his meds without anyone knowing it and replaced them with more socially acceptable medications. Acceptable, at least, in the rock and roll world.

First, it was just grass. Then grass and liquor. Then Valium. By the time he reached heroin, he was a working musician, so people looked the other way. In the end, he had a near-fatal overdose, so he pulled back.

Now that he was older, he had a perspective on his "gift" and had learned to live with it. He tried to avoid places where the divide between our world and theirs was the thinnest. When he couldn't avoid places like that, he ignored his "curse" the best he could and got by with a little grass and an occasional drink. It had been a roller-coaster life so far, and it had taken its toll on him emotionally and physically.

Roger felt the cold rain soaking completely through his hoodie, and he realized he had been standing outside for longer than he had thought. He stepped back inside the hall and closed the door.

This might be a place where the divide between the worlds was thin, but he would ignore this. Pretend it didn't happen. He was going to get back in the car and keep going to Salt Lake City.

Four

Lucinda was gone, and Kat was busy busing her dishes when Roger came back into the diner. Kat glanced over and registered his distracted mood. He picked up his soup at the counter and painted on a smile for her.

"Hey, thanks," he said.

Kat came over, wiping her hands. "Sure," she said. She tossed the rag under the counter and shot a look back at him. "You okay?"

Roger nodded. "Yeah. Tired, but okay."

"We got sleeping rooms here if you need one," she offered.

"Nah, I gotta be in Salt Lake in the morning." He backed toward the front door.

"Well, drive careful."

"Yeah, thanks again." He pushed out the door.

Kat watched after him for a moment; there was definitely something going on with him.

Outside, Roger paused under the awning and zipped up his hoodie. He had to get back to Lilly, but he needed to do something else first; try as he might to ignore his experience in the hallway, it had unnerved him. He looked around and spotted an alcove nearby that had a clear view of his car but was hidden from the diner. He pulled his hood on and ducked out into the rain.

Kat watched Roger hurry toward the alcove and duck out of sight. What the hell was he up to? She strolled up to the window and craned to the side, trying to see where he had gone. It was no use. She couldn't see the alcove from inside. She looked back at the dining room. It was just the family in the corner booth now, their raincoats still dripping, hung over the booth next to them, and Bart was in the kitchen doing prep work. Kat looked at her watch, then crossed back around behind the counter.

Outside, Roger faded back into the alcove. He looked over at his car, parked and locked safely just a few feet away, and dug into his pocket. He took out a joint, fired it up, and took a deep hit.

This is what he needed now. It was the only way to block the shit out. He exhaled slowly as he scanned the parking lot around him. Not much had changed. He saw several long-haul rigs and the family's minivan, then his eyes locked on a muddy old tanker truck, several yards away.

Seated behind the dark, dirty windshield was a gaunt truck driver with haunted, hollow eyes. Steam rose up in front of him as he poured himself a cup of something hot, probably coffee from a Thermos. Before Roger could look away again, the trucker looked up and stared right back at Roger.

Roger was startled, but he didn't look away. The moment became odd and a bit creepy. Then, the driver snapped off his dome light and disappeared into the darkness of the cab.

Roger took another hit off his joint. The faint sounds of sex drifted to him over the drumming rain. He looked the other direction and saw a double trailer-truck. Through the partially open shade, Roger could see Lucinda grinding away on top of some unseen trucker. She arched her back and thrust out her perky, pale breasts; the man's hands slid up from below and grabbed them firmly. Rough, old hands. Black dried oil under the nails. They squeezed hard, but Lucinda didn't react; she just kept riding away with a distant look in her eyes and her best "fuck me hard" expression frozen on her face.

Roger couldn't help but wonder what was going on in Lucinda's head. Was she counting her fee? Or was she counting time until he came? The dirty hands gripped harder; Roger half expected them to leave oily marks on her milky white tits. God, this place was weird.

"I hear she's cheap, but her blow jobs really suck."

Roger looked over, startled. Kat was standing right behind him in the alcove.

"And I don't mean that in a good way," she added with a smile, and reached over for the joint.

Roger hesitated, passed the joint to her. "Bad, huh? Then you can definitely count me out," he smiled back.

Kat took a deep hit, exhaling long and slow. She studied him for a moment in silence, then said, "You know, you looked a little freaked when you came back from the bathroom. Cockroaches a little much for you?"

"No, didn't see any roaches," he said, before taking another hit.

"Too bad. They're actually kinda like family. I've got names for most of them."

Roger chuckled, passed the joint back to her. She started to take another hit, then hesitated. "So, what then? You run into one of our local freakazoids back there?"

Roger shook his head. "No."

Kat pressed on. "Well, you don't strike me as a dude who gets put off his game if someone doesn't courtesy flush. What was it?"

Roger assessed his new friend for a moment; she wasn't going to let this go. He'd been in this conversation a million times before, and it always went one way or the other. He had learned to inch his way into the topic and gauge how people were responding. If the explanation went south, he'd have to laugh it off and pretend he was bullshitting them, or, if they were open to the idea, things would be fairly cool. Most of the time he could tell how the person would react; sometimes he was surprised. It seemed like a pretty good bet Kat would be cool, so he shrugged. "I...I had an encounter," he said.

Kat looked at him, puzzled. "An encounter. Okay, now we're getting somewhere. Doesn't sound good, but at least we're getting somewhere."

Roger studied her a little longer, then decided to just drop it out there cold. "I'm a sensitive."

Kat held on to this a moment in her head, trying to digest exactly what he was saying. "A...sensitive," she repeated.

"I can see things a lot of people can't. Ghosts. Spirits. Apparitions."

Kat brightened. "Residual energy stuff?"

Roger had read her right. She was just new age enough to buy into it. Either that, or her parents were new agers, and she had grown up around it. "Sure. Residual energy stuff. That works too."

Kat gazed up at him. "No shit?"

"No shit," Roger said firmly.

There was a long beat, and a smile spread across Kat's face. "Y'know, this is, like, cool. Very cool."

"Cool? No. Not like cool. Not like cool at all. Not when you've been living with it as long as I have. It fucking sucks." He held up the joint, displaying it for her. "So, you do what you have to do to numb it out."

Kat grew genuinely interested. "Weed stops you from seeing things?"

"No, not completely, but it helps. Stronger shit works way better, but hey. I went down the heroin highway, and it wasn't leading me anywhere except rehab. So, yeah. Now all I've got is the weed and a prescription for anxiety."

Kat took a moment to absorb all this before speaking. "Dude, I always thought this place was haunted."

Roger smiled; her limited understanding of his hell was so innocently charming he couldn't help himself. "It's not just here. It's everywhere. Usually there's a reason behind it."

Kat jumped in eagerly. "Right. Like when someone left something unfinished, or they died unexpectedly. Or they were really happy someplace, or really sad."

Roger took a moment to just look at her; she was a bit deeper into this than he thought, but still naïve. "I'm guessing someone's been watching *Ghost Hunters* on The Travel Channel."

Kat smiled proudly. "Just, like, every chance I can."

Of course. *Ghost Hunters*. Those idiotic jerks with their night vision cameras who locked themselves inside haunted houses at night. It was like saying you felt like you'd been to Switzerland after riding the Matterhorn at Disneyland.

Roger shook his head. "Yeah, well that's all bullshit. They think they got it down, but they don't. Half the time it's someone farting, and they think they've recorded a spectral voice." He held up the joint for her again. "You want?"

Kat shook her head. "I wish. But I gotta go back to work. Believe it or not, my job can be a real bitch if I'm too faded. Trust me, I've tried."

Roger stubbed out the roach, pocketed it. "Yeah, I gotta keep going too."

And there they were again, in the middle of another of their lingering, awkward moments. But this time, things took a quick turn. Kat leaned up and kissed him impulsively.

Roger was taken by surprise. He was about to back off, but then it became effortless, and comfortable, and filled with energy all at the same time. He pulled her closer. The kiss grew deep and slow, and they were both lost in it.

Kat pulled away after several moments, whispered breathlessly, "Fuck."

Roger's entire body lit up with a surge that overpowered anything he was feeling from the weed.

Kat brushed her hair out of her eyes and nervously dug into her apron. They were both wrestling with what had just happened, and the moment became more awkward than all of the others they had shared combined.

She took out a napkin with her phone number already written on it and held it out, feeling more than a little embarrassed. "Here," she said. "I was only planning to humiliate myself a little bit."

Roger looked down at the napkin and smiled. "No, no. This is great. I'll call you."

"Sure, right. Or I'll see you in Vegas. Whatever." Kat was feeling so uncool that she just wanted to get out of there as fast as she could. "I gotta go."

She turned to leave, but Roger caught her arm. "Hey," he said softly. Kat turned back and met his gaze. There was warmth and reassurance in his eyes. "I'll be driving back through here Monday. See you then."

Kat felt her awkwardness melt away; she smiled involuntarily. "Cool."

Roger let her go. She gave him a final look, then hurried off into the rain.

Roger watched her disappear into the diner door. Yes, this place was definitely not ordinary, Roger decided. He pulled up his hood and ducked out of the alcove. He thought belatedly of Lilly. While he had been absorbed with Kat in the alcove, neither of them had been looking directly at the car. But what could happen? It had been a matter of a minute or two, and they were so close to the car, they would have noticed any disturbance. The car doors were locked, in any case.

The rain had decided not to let up. Not even a little. Roger hurried over to his car, fumbled with his keys as he wiped the water from his eyes. Of course the car was still locked. He managed to get the key in the lock and twist it.

He slid in behind the wheel and closed the door. He took a deep breath, pulled the hood off his head. He carefully set the soggy bag with his soup on the seat next to him and pulled out the napkin.

He smiled when he looked at Kat's number, then carefully folded the napkin and tucked it into his pocket. "All right, Lilly," Roger whispered, so he would not wake his daughter. "No more stops. Straight on through to Salt Lake City."

He started the car and adjusted the wiper speed, again cursing the bulky wipers. He slipped the car into reverse, looked over his shoulder to back up, and stopped cold. The back seat was empty, except for the blanket.

Lilly was gone.

Six

Roger slammed on the brakes and leaped out of the car. He shoved the seat forward, tossed the blanket aside, and looked around the back seat. This couldn't be happening. She had to be hiding. He looked on the floor of both the back seat and the front passenger seat, but there was no Lilly, no pink rabbit.

Roger spun back, scanned the parking lot. "Lilly?" he yelled.

No response.

He spotted a middle-aged man over at the gas pump. "Hey!"

It was futile; the man couldn't hear him over the wash of rain. Roger slammed the car door and ran over to him.

The man looked up, startled, as Roger approached. "Excuse me! Hey, did you see a little girl get out of my car over there?"

The man looked over at Roger's Mustang and shook his head. "Not since I've been here," he said.

Roger spun around, squinted out into the wet darkness. Nothing seemed out of place—just the trucks coming and going. His stomach tightened as his panic rose. He yelled desperately, "Lilly!"

Inside the diner, Kat was pouring coffee for the adults at the family's table when she looked out and saw Roger running away from the gas pump and back toward his car. She could tell there was something wrong. She dropped the coffeepot off at the busing station and hurried to the front door.

Roger was running past as Kat stepped outside. "Roger!" she yelled. Roger saw her and cut over to the awning, out of breath. "What's the—?" Kat started.

"You watched my car the whole time, didn't you?" he panted.

"Yeah, of course. What's wrong?"

"Lilly. My daughter. She's missing."

"Missing?"

"Yes. She's gone. I went back to the car and she wasn't there."

"But I—"

"You didn't see anyone go near the car, did you?"

Kat shook her head "No. No one. And I didn't see her get out, either."

Bart yelled from the diner behind Kat, "Order's up!"

Kat shot an annoyed look back at Bart. "Hold on a…." She looked back at Roger, but he was already running toward his car.

"Kat, come on!" Bart yelled insistently.

Kat sighed, frustrated, and reluctantly went back inside.

Roger raced up to his car and looked around again. Kat had been watching her while he had been in the hallway and the men's room, and they hadn't been in the alcove more than five minutes. Even if she had noticed the adults' inattention and purposely slipped out the far door of the car in the rain, which was unlikely, Lilly couldn't have gotten far in five minutes. He looked over at the trucks parked closest to his car. Someone had to have seen something, he decided, and raced over to the nearest one.

It was a glossy maroon-colored rig with the lights on in the cab. He pounded on the door. "Hello?"

The door popped open and a woman appeared. She wasn't at all what Roger expected to find in a trucker. She was in her early 60s, with short salt-and-pepper hair and kind, matronly eyes—the picture-perfect, favorite-aunt type. "What's wrong, honey?" she asked.

"I'm looking for my daughter. She's seven, brunette, in pink pajamas and a blue sweatshirt. She was in my car over there." Roger waved his hand at his Mustang.

The woman squinted out into the rainy darkness, then looked back at Roger. "I've been here about an hour, but I haven't seen any little ones out in this rain," she said.

Roger sighed anxiously, looked around at the other nearby trucks. "Shit."

"Oh, dear. You don't know where she is?

"No. No, someone was watching the car, but my daughter managed to get out anyway," Roger explained, trying to contain his frustration.

"Oh, no." the woman said with honest worry in her voice. "I'm sorry, honey, I haven't seen her, but I will—" Roger was gone before she could finish. She watched him dart over to the pearly cream-colored rig next door with its large sleeper cab.

Roger pounded on the door. Waited. After a moment, he could hear the faint muffled voice of a man inside. "Momma… someone's at the door."

The door opened a crack, and another woman peered out. She was in her late 40s, muscular, with spiked white hair and gold-capped teeth. "Yeah?" she asked warily.

"Hi," Roger said. "My daughter's missing. She's seven, brown hair—"

A man's voice called out from behind the middle-aged woman. "Who is it, Momma?"

The woman barked back, "I got it, Daniel!"

Daniel, a soft-spoken eighteen-year-old, peered

out from behind his mother. He had a thin, delicate nose, full lips and large, doe-like eyes. He would have been a beautiful woman if he hadn't been a man.

"Someone's lost?" he asked.

"I told you, I got it," his mother snapped, annoyed. Daniel retreated out of sight. The woman looked back at Roger. "We ain't seen no one."

Roger peered anxiously into the cab behind her, trying for a better look, but he couldn't see much. This woman trucker didn't have the warm tone in her voice that the other woman had. "Are you sure? She was in my car over there, and—"

"We been watchin' TV. Ain't seen anything. Sorry." She cut him off, then added with a forced smile, "But we'll keep a look out." She snapped the door closed.

Roger spun around desperately. There was one more nearby truck, a beat-up old Mack with Georgia plates.

Roger raced over, pounded on the door. A heavyset man in his late 40s shoved the door open. He had deep creases in his slightly bloated face, one eye that looked slightly off to the left, and he wheezed with every effort. "What's up?" he growled.

"Hi. I wanted to know if you saw a little girl, my daughter. She's brunette, seven."

"You lost your kid?" the man interrupted sharply.

"Yes. I mean, she was in my car, right there," Roger pointed.

The man's watery eyes glanced at the car, then back at Roger. "She was by herself?"

"No. Someone was watching her, but she somehow got out of my car."

"Jesus Lord," the big man wheezed, irritated. He

was doing everything he could to hide his obvious frustration with Roger, or with any parent who would let this happen.

"Look, I'm just trying to find out if you saw her." Roger offered defensively.

"You look inside the truck stop?"

But Roger's attention was diverted to the sleeper cab behind the man. There were a couple of Confederate flags strung up, and a gun rack with several rifles. Roger looked back at the big, asthmatic man, a little rattled by what he was seeing behind him. "Huh?"

"The truck stop. The diner. Gift shop," the driver snapped insistently. He had given up trying to temper his irritation.

"No, I was in there when she—" Roger started to explain but stopped. Why the fuck should he care what this fat old asshole thought? He turned away. "Fuck it."

The big man shook his head and closed the door. Roger steadied himself on the running board. His whole world was spinning out of control. A complete disaster was unfolding, and with no sign that it was going to let up.

He looked from the front of the diner to the repair garage and truck wash in the distance behind it, then back over to the diner. His eyes strayed to the dark highway.

Nausea swept up his throat; his heart skipped. The highway. Dear God, please no.

Roger ran flat out across the parking lot. The cold rain stung his red face like needles, and his lungs ached by the time he reached the edge of the road.

A truck sailed past, blasting its horn. A shock of cold, muddy water splashed over Roger. He recoiled, shielded himself, shouted, "Fuck!"

He staggered back, wiping the water from his eyes. He spit several times, trying to expel the grit from his teeth. "Motherfu…."

Roger managed to clear his eyes and squinted out across the dark road. That's when he saw it, a pale body lying in the ditch on the other side.

Roger screamed, horrified. "Lilly!"

He bolted out into the highway. A car blasted its horn and swerved to miss him. Roger raced blindly through the swirling rain in the car's wake. He reached the other side as passing headlights from another truck swung by. The pale body was a dead deer. Maggots swarmed the wet innards that spilled out onto the soaking asphalt.

Roger reeled from the sickening sight. He coughed and gagged, nearly vomiting. This was hell, no doubt about it. An unending nightmare that he couldn't wake up from. And the end was nowhere in sight.

Seven

Kat was serving the family their dinner when Roger bolted back inside the diner. He was flushed and out of breath. He made a cursory check of the diner then charged off toward the adjoining gift shop.

Kat set down the last plate of food on the family's table and called after him. "Roger!" He ignored her.

Roger made a loop through the shadowy gift shop, past the dusty shelves of travel aids and crappy cheap toys. If Lilly were here, she would be sitting in one of the aisles playing with some little plastic dog. The animals were always her favorites. If they ever got separated in a toy store, he would always find her lost in some make-believe game of talking animals. She created long, intricate scenarios that played out the story lines from her favorite DVDs, usually *The Lion King* or *Balto*. Roger would then begin a protracted negotiation on how many of the little animals she could buy, and which ones. But not this time. Lilly was nowhere to be seen. The gift shop was empty.

Roger darted out of the shop, crossed over to the hallway door, and threw it open. The long, eerie hallway was deserted. Roger gave a look in both directions. "Lilly!" His voice echoed in the emptiness.

No response. Just the buzzing of the fluorescents and the dripping of the rainwater into the buckets. Roger took off down the hall, rattling the knobs and pounding on the shower and sleeping room doors as he went "Lilly! Are you in here?"

Nothing. He reached the men's room and ducked inside.

Roger raced down the row of stalls, banging them

open and looking inside. They were all empty. Roger spun around, catching his breath, his mind racing. Then he took off again for the door.

He bolted back out into the hallway and ran headlong into Kat. "Hey!" She recoiled, startled.

"I can't find her. She's nowhere around," Roger panted desperately.

Kat recovered, took a deep breath, and did her best to remain calm. "Roger, she's got to be here someplace. She must've got out the driver's side of the car that I couldn't see. She probably came looking for you on her own and got lost."

Roger didn't hear Kat's attempt to reassure him. He pushed past her, shoving open the women's room door. Kat followed him inside.

Roger raced down the row of stalls, banging them open as he went. "Lilly?" He reached the end. The place was empty. "Fuck! How could she just disappear?"

Kat approached him, still trying to remain calm. "All right," she said. "We'll find her. There're a lot of places she could be. This is a big place. Let me tell Bart so he can take over in the diner, and I'll help you look."

But Roger wasn't listening again. He sped out the door. "Roger!" Kat called after him.

Roger hurried down the long hallway, weaving around the buckets of rainwater. He reached the back door with the small windowpane and shoved it open.

He stepped outside, scanned the wet darkness, and cupped his hands on either side of his mouth. "LILLY!" he screamed into the cold night.

The drumming rain swallowed his voice. He looked over at a shadowy junkyard beyond the cyclone fence and yelled for her again. But nothing came back to him. No small cry. No "Daddy, I'm here." Nothing.

Roger pressed on, determined. He cut around the

side of the truck stop complex to the repair garage.

A strange, pale flickering light emanated from inside the barn-like metal structure. Roger stepped around to the front of the building; the garage doors were open.

The mechanic he had met at the gas pumps in front of the diner when he first arrived was seated at a workbench beyond the service bays in back. A black spark shield covered his head, and he was working an arc welder. "Excuse me!" Roger yelled.

The man didn't hear him over the crackling and buzzing. Roger stepped through the open doors and carefully made his way across the greasy concrete floor past a large, dangling engine-hoist chain. Boxes of parts and supplies lined the walls, and closed doors led to what must be storage rooms or office space.

As he grew closer, he could see that the mechanic was welding a crankshaft onto a sculpture made of various discarded engine parts. The sculpture was strangely elegant and almost organic-looking. It seemed alive as it danced and flickered in the smoke and flashing light from the arc welder.

"Hey!" Roger yelled.

This time the man stopped but didn't turn off his welder. He looked up, his black welder's mask still over his face.

"I'm looking for my daughter. Seven, brown hair. Have you seen her back here anywhere?" Roger asked.

The mechanic paused for a moment before shaking his head. Roger waited for something more, but he looked back at his sculpture and resumed his welding. Roger considered pressing the point but thought the better of it.

He turned away and looked out the open garage doors. The truck wash building loomed nearby.

Roger ducked back out into the rain and hurried over to the cavernous building. He stepped into the truck wash entrance and peered down the long, shadowy tunnel filled with idle hydraulics. "Lilly?" he yelled.

Roger made his way down the corridor, past the massive, lifeless brushes and shammies. He paused halfway down, considered the eerie, shadowy tunnel. This was a waste of time. She'd never go in here. Not in a million years.

Roger deliberated his next move, and that was when he heard it—several truck engines rumbling to life in the parking lot out front.

* * *

Roger raced around the side of the complex in time to see several trucks clicking on their headlights; their air brakes popped and hissed. The family from the diner was piling into their minivan. Everyone was on the move at once, for some reason.

Kat appeared at the diner doorway. "Roger!" she called.

"What's going on?" Roger asked as he cut over to her.

"Word just went out that the top of the grade is going to get snowed in. This is the last shot at getting over the pass tonight."

Roger watched the row of trucks getting ready to leave. Their occupants were the only remaining witnesses who might have seen something.

"Shit," he swore, and took off.

Kat watched him make a beeline toward the first truck as it headed out to the highway. "Hey! Roger, be careful!"

Roger waved his arms and cut in front of the first truck as it rumbled toward the on-ramp. The massive beast slammed on its brakes and shuddered to a stop. Roger cut around to the cab and leaped up onto the side step. The annoyed, heavily tattooed driver rolled down his window. "What the fuck are you—?"

"I'm looking for a little girl. My daughter," Roger panted as he craned his neck and looked into the cab.

"I haven't seen any kids. Now come on, get off my truck," the driver shot back.

Roger hopped off the side step, and the truck lurched away with a grinding of gears. Roger cut over to the cab of the second truck in line.

The grizzled old man behind the wheel already had his window down when Roger leaped up onto the side step. "You outta your fucking mind?" the old guy growled. "You're gonna get yourself killed!"

Roger desperately scanned the inside of the cab. "I'm looking for my daughter. She's brunette, seven—"

The truck behind them started blasting its horn.

"I ain't seen no one," the old trucker snarled.

Roger leaped off the side step and raced over to the last truck. But this one didn't stop. It blasted its horn and kept rolling.

Roger ran up alongside it, yelling at the wiry 30-something man behind the wheel. "Hey! Hey asshole!" he shouted. But the truck roared out onto the on-ramp, leaving Roger behind in the pouring rain.

Roger staggered to a stop, catching his breath. He turned and looked back at the parking lot. Four trucks had decided to sit out the storm at the truck stop. One was the cream-colored rig with the pearly finish that belonged to the spiky-haired woman and her son Daniel. Another was the maroon-colored rig that belonged to the amiable favorite-aunt type woman. The third was the beat-up old Mack with the Georgia plates that belonged to the man with the Confederate flag and the guns, and the fourth one....

Roger wiped the water from his eyes and focused in on the fourth remaining truck. It was the muddy old tanker truck, the truck with the cab he had looked into earlier and seen the gaunt-looking driver with the hollow, sunken eyes staring back.

Roger cut back across the parking lot, heading straight for the foreboding old tanker. All the lights were off in the cab. He stepped up to the door and knocked.

Thunder rumbled in the black, wet sky overhead. Roger knocked again. No answer. He climbed up onto the side step and peered into the window. The dark and mud were impervious. He used his hand to try to wipe the mud from the cab's windows, but it streaked and smeared across the opaque glass.

Roger gave up and stepped back down. He crossed around the front of the cab, carefully scanning the old truck as he went. There was something out of place about it; it wasn't kept up like the others. It was as if the driver didn't care.

Roger considered his options. If the driver wasn't inside his truck, then he had to be in the truck stop somewhere. Roger would at least have to track the driver down and question him the way he had the others. One thing was certain; he would have to keep a close eye on this truck.

Roger turned away and was about to head back to the truck stop when a flicker of lightning lit up the turbulent sky. Roger hesitated; something caught his eye in the pale glow.

He looked down at the front wheel well of the tanker truck. Strange, thin, wet strands hung from underneath. Roger kneeled. He reached behind the muddy tire and pulled at one of the strands. It slipped away from the greasy axle. Roger held it close for a better look. It was human hair, clotted with blood and bits of pulpy scalp clinging to the ends.

Roger swallowed dryly; his heart began to thunder in his chest. He dropped to his hands and knees and looked up under the wheel well. The rainwater dripped down through the oily engine. Roger waited for his eyes to adjust to the new level of darkness, and he saw something else caught up in the struts. It was pale, soft, and irregular, with something dark hanging from it.

Roger scooted farther under the truck. The closer he got to the hanging object, the more details he could make out. The dark hanging shape was the cuff from a torn pair of jeans, but there was more than just fabric there.

He squinted as he scooted closer and reached out. The second he touched it, he knew what the fabric contained. Human flesh. Cold, dead. An ankle. A toe. It was a human foot severed at the ankle; the blood was thick and oozing from the tattered flesh.

Roger withdrew his hand, startled. He wrenched around, started to squirm away on his stomach. He was almost out from underneath when another flicker of lightning flashed overhead, illuminating the greasy undercarriage. A human face was in front of him. It was a head, severed at the shoulders, mutilated and bloody, and it was caught in a corner of the tight space. The body had obviously been ripped away from it.

Roger cried out, horrified, and the dead eyes on the severed head snapped open and stared right at Roger. Its mouth dropped, oozing blood, and it began gurgling in desperate pain, "Hel...help me...."

Roger froze in horror at the bizarre sight, and he closed his eyes tight. This had to be one of his visions.

He remained for a moment with his eyes clamped shut; then he took a steady, deep breath. He opened his eyes again. Sure enough, the mutilated head was gone. There was nothing under the truck but engine parts and grease.

Roger let out a long, steady breath. He reached up, grabbed the outer edge of the fender, and pulled himself out from under the truck. He staggered to his feet.

WHAP! A hand slapped down on Roger's shoulder and spun him around.

Roger came face to face with the gaunt trucker, who was brandishing a heavy lug wrench.

"What the fuck are you doing under my rig?" the driver asked angrily.

"Get your hand off me, asshole." Roger shoved the man's hand off his shoulder.

The gaunt trucker lunged back at Roger, cracking him in the ribs with the wrench. Roger smashed back against the fender, clutching his aching side. He looked up and saw the trucker rearing back with the wrench for another swing.

Roger rolled out of the way just in time. The wrench clanged down onto the fender. The trucker spun around, came for Roger again. This time Roger leaped right at him, tackling him to the wet asphalt. The lug wrench clattered out of the trucker's hand and went skittering under the engine compartment.

Roger cracked the trucker across the jaw, shoved him aside. He scrambled over and grabbed the wrench. He was coming up with it when a voice yelled from the darkness, "Freeze! Don't move!"

Roger looked up and saw a highway patrolman

standing several yards away, with his pistol trained dead on Roger.

Eight

Ben Clark, an African-American highway patrolman in his mid-30s, sat at a corner booth across from Roger and Kat. He had surprised even himself at how patient he had been for the last forty minutes. First, he had managed to diffuse the conflict outside with Roger and the trucker, then he had separated them, and now he was focusing on Roger's long, twisting story.

Ben prided himself on withholding judgment until he had all the facts in front of him. He knew that most of his buddies in law enforcement claimed that they did this, but in the end they were only human, and they usually judged people on what they looked like and how they acted; Ben had seen it happen a million times.

Roger had looked like trouble with his rocker tattoos, hair, and clothes, but Ben had soon discovered that Roger was just a frightened father who had lost his daughter. Ben couldn't help but sympathize; he would be out of his mind if he had lost sight of his little boy for as long as Roger had been missing Lilly. So, Ben had taken things a step at a time, and now he was trying to get everything written down as accurately as possible.

For his part, Roger was doing everything he could to hold it together. He looked anxiously out the window at the old tanker truck as he relayed his side of things. "I saw him after I went to the bathroom," he said. "He knew I left Lilly in the car. I'm telling you, that creep out there is the one you should be talking to."

Ben looked up from his notepad. "I'll get to him,

don't worry. He's not going anywhere." He gestured to the trucker's keys on the table next to him, then looked over at Kat. "So, the entire time Roger was gone, you didn't see anyone come near his car?"

"No one."

"And you watched it the whole time?"

Kat took an anxious breath and nodded, but it was getting harder every time she went over it. After all, it had been her responsibility all along. No one had come out and blamed her for anything, but it didn't matter. The guilt had been nagging at her, and now she felt it was about to overwhelm her. "I mean it was raining pretty hard. I guess it's possible I...." She trailed off, feeling nauseated, then took a breath and forced herself to say what had probably been obvious all along. "I might have missed Lilly getting out, or even someone coming up to the car."

Kat trailed off into silence. There. She had said it herself. She had thought that it might be better this way, but it wasn't. She felt sick about it. Lilly had probably left the car while it was her responsibility to watch it, and now she was missing. Kat looked down, unable to look in Roger's direction. She didn't have to see the expression on his face to know what he was feeling.

Ben referred to his notes to find a name Roger had mentioned earlier. "Zoe. Your ex-wife," he said to Roger.

"What about her?"

"You said you picked your daughter up from her house in Las Vegas. Why was she there if you have sole custody?"

A simple question, but Roger felt an old familiar feeling creep up on him. It was the nagging guilt that had colored his entire life. "I...I didn't have a choice. I had a gig in L.A., and I couldn't take her with me."

"And you don't think there's any chance Zoe could have followed you here and taken your daughter?"

Roger shook his head. "Zoe? No way. She doesn't want anything to do with my daughter. She's in love with her pipe. That's pretty much what you get when you meet your wife in rehab." As soon as the bitter words were out of his mouth, Roger felt awkward. Could he sum up such an important part of his life so quickly and callously? He used to think it was so much more complex.

Roger had loved Zoe when they met. They had connected. Not just through the shared misery of dependency, but through a shared desire to get better. They had found strength together, and Roger began to believe that that strength was going to be enough to turn things around. Of course, it hadn't been. Not for her. Not for Zoe.

Ben referred to his notes again for another question. "What about this boyfriend of hers, Jack Murphy?"

Roger felt a deeper pain stab into him this time. His whole life was being dragged out and put on an autopsy table in front of him. The God's truth was that Jack was a motherfucker. At first, Roger had held out hope that Zoe would turn things around for herself, but then she met Jack. Jack the dealer. The crackhead who thought he was a gangster because he got his shit from some low-level mob connection in Vegas. So how much of this do I try to explain? Roger thought. He decided to downplay it. "Look, they're both users, and they're both seriously messed up," he said.

Roger looked at Ben then and saw the officer looking at him a bit differently. It wasn't the look of a cop. It was the look of a father. It hit Roger then how fucked up his entire life was. "Okay, I know. I shouldn't have left Lilly there, but I didn't have a choice. Anyway, she was fine when I picked her up." He didn't mention the fact that Lilly had been waiting for him by herself, with no sign of any adult presence save the lights and the television.

Ben considered this. It was times like this when he found it hard not to pass judgment. He managed to let it go, and he looked back down at his notes. "All right, I think I've got everything here. I'm going to go ahead and issue an Amber Alert on your daughter. We've had a lot of luck finding missing children with the system in the past."

"A lot? This happens a lot?"

Ben flipped his notepad closed and tucked it in his jacket. "The sad truth is, it's not that unusual for people to go missing out here. It's a transient world on the Interstates. People come and go." Ben stood up, saw the concern on Roger and Kat's faces, and added, "But like I said, she hasn't been missing long, and we've had a lot of luck using the Amber Alert system."

Ben grabbed his hat and turned to leave, but then he remembered another question. "What exactly did you see under the truck out there?" he asked Roger.

The seemingly innocent question hung in the air for a moment. Roger felt Kat's eyes on him, and he looked over at her. She had been careful in her answers to Ben's questions. She had not mentioned the joint they had smoked together or anything about their conversation about his "gift."

Roger considered his answer. He knew the creepy bastard out there was guilty. Very guilty. But Roger couldn't tell Ben exactly how he knew. He couldn't tell Ben that every time he had an encounter with the other side, it was always at the place where someone had lost his or her life. In this case, someone had been run over by that truck. Sure, maybe it was years ago and someone else was driving, but Roger doubted it. He had a feeling about that creepy asshole, and usually his feelings were right.

Roger decided he had to play it off. There was no choice. He had to keep things focused on finding Lilly. "Well, I thought I saw something that looked like…like a person's shirt or something."

"A shirt?" Ben asked, puzzled. This seemed like an unusual detail.

Ben's reaction threw Roger. He was distracted and hadn't thought it through well enough. The shirt was too strange. He had to backpedal. "Well, yeah. I mean, I don't know. It looked like something was tangled in there, but it was nothing."

Ben considered this for a moment, then moved away, "Stay put," he told both of them. "I'll be back." He zipped up his jacket, pushed out the diner door.

Roger and Kat watched as he headed over to the tanker truck.

"Russell Fields," said a voice.

Roger and Kat looked up and saw Bart, the cook, who had come out of the kitchen.

"The guy driving the tanker truck? You know him?" Roger asked.

Bart nodded and held out his hand to Roger. "Bart Corrigan," he said, and Roger reciprocated, shaking the man's hand. "Fields has been coming through here for years," Bart said.

"I've only seen him a few times heading to the bathroom," Kat said. "He never told me his name and I sure as shit wasn't going to ask him. Dude is a fucking troll."

"He's a loner, that's for sure," Bart added. "But I never saw him cause no trouble or nothing."

Roger looked back out at the tanker truck. His expression grew dark. "Doesn't mean he wasn't up to it."

Nine

Ben leaned in the open door of the old tanker truck cab, looking up at Russell Fields, who sat patiently behind the wheel. In the dim yellow cab light, Russell seemed rather ordinary, but at the same time, he was strangely out of place. He wore a plaid work shirt and patched jeans. Ben's first thought when he saw him was about the patches on his knees. Who patches their jeans anymore? It was something Ben hadn't seen since he was a little boy. Ben had also carefully searched the truck and hadn't found anything out of the ordinary, just a lot of empty cups and plastic wrappers. Ben had decided Russell's gaunt face and rail-thin body were because he lived on a steady stream of beef jerky and coffee, and probably other stimulants that were less than legal.

But there was also an undeniably strange, timeless quality, about him, like he could have stepped out of the pages of *The Grapes of Wrath*. An Okie heading from the dust bowl during the Great Depression. If he had been seeing this in a black-and-white movie, Ben thought, it would all make more sense.

The rain had slowed to a light drizzle, and the Utah night air was becoming bone-numbing cold. Ben's breath came out in pale puffs of mist as he spoke. "And you hadn't talked to him or seen him before you found him under your truck?" he asked Fields.

"No sir. I told you, I was just protecting my rig. My life depends on this thing. I don't let no one get near it unless I'm right there with them," Russell answered.

"I understand." And Ben did understand. This was the part that seemed so ordinary about Russell. He made sense. He seemed earnest.

Ben took another glance around the cab, then handed Russell back his driver's license and his keys. "All right, look," he said to the driver. "If you're going to be staying here for the night, keep out of his way. He's got a missing daughter and he's upset."

"Of course, sir. I sure will." Russell nodded.

And that was it. There was nothing else to be done. Ben had found nothing illegal in Russell defending his property; there was nothing suspicious in or around the truck, and no reason to suspect Russell of abducting Lilly.

Ben closed the rig door and folded his notepad. He looked around at the other nearby trucks, pulled his collar up against the biting cold, and was about to head to the next truck when he hesitated. One more thing.

He clicked on his flashlight, kneeled and looked under the truck. He moved the beam slowly across the greasy underside of the engine compartment. Nothing out of the ordinary.

Inside the diner, Roger watched intently out the window.

"What is he doing now?" Kat asked. She was seated on the other side and didn't have the same view that Roger could.

"Just looking around underneath the truck," Roger answered, and kept watching.

Kat gazed at Roger for a moment in silence. She wanted to say something more to him about everything she was feeling, but it wasn't the right time. Not now. Not yet. But she would, she promised herself, when the time was right.

* * *

Back outside in the cold parking lot, a faint gasp and a low moan drifted from inside the pearly cream-colored rig. Ben was still looking under the tanker truck, and he was too far away to hear it. Too far away to hear what was going on inside the sleeper cab.

Ida Consiglio calmly took a drag off a filter-less Camel as she gazed into the sleeper side of the cab. Her son's groans, interspersed with sharp gasps of pain, filled the cab. The windows were steamed up, and the cab was smoky and humid.

Ida exhaled a cloud of smoke. "Don't let up on him, honey," she growled. "Don't you dare go easy." She was looking at Lucinda in the bed, dominating Daniel with a strap-on from behind.

The low-rent prostitute nodded breathlessly to Ida and continued her sodomy. Lucinda had done many things in her short but extensive life as a truck stop hooker, but this had come as a surprise. At first, she thought Ida was engaging her for Daniel as a kinky gift from mother to son. It had happened before to Lucinda, but it was usually a father who bought her for his son. The fathers usually ended up taking her when she had finished with their sons, but usually they were generous with the additional fee.

But this. This was different. Ida had negotiated the deal for her son, and Lucinda had accepted. When she had climbed into the cab, she had found Daniel already naked in bed waiting. The first clue was his expression. He looked scared. At first, Lucinda thought it was one of those virgin things; Mom had hired her to pop her son's cherry. Thinking this, Lucinda had then gone out of her way to be nice to Daniel. She smiled seductively and promised to go easy.

But it all began to turn when Ida told her that Daniel wasn't a virgin. Lucinda couldn't figure out why he looked so scared, until Ida took out the strap-on.

Lucinda hesitated when Ida told her what she wanted her to do to her son. But Ida didn't back down; she even became a bit intimidating. She insisted that it was what Daniel wanted, even though Daniel remained silent the whole time. And that's when the rationalizing began—a process familiar to Lucinda.

A year ago, Lucinda had ended up at a motel between the truck stop and Vegas after her boyfriend drove off without her. He had taken her last few dollars and the rest of their crystal meth. She was flat broke and strung out bad. She had to get right again, and a hand job for the guy at the gas station next door was the solution. Twenty bucks. He took her into the bathroom in back, dropped his pants, and she jerked him off. It was over in about six minutes and she had twenty bucks. Not so bad. Just a hand job.

But twenty dollars is just twenty dollars. She could get fifty for a blow job. Same six minutes, different deed. Fifty bucks. And so it went. Blow jobs, straight sex, 50-50. Two guys at once. A girl and a guy. And anal. Finally anal. That was three hundred. She had to use amyl-nitrate poppers to relax herself, use lots of lube, and it took longer, but still it was three hundred dollars.

Now it all seemed the same to Lucinda. Just one more thing to do. One more thing to rationalize. The sex. The money. The meth. The merry-go-round that Lucinda found herself on.

What she was doing with Daniel Consiglio now was another twist on something she had done a few times before; men liked her strap-on work. She was quite good at it, but she had never done it with the man's mother watching.

Daniel grimaced, his eyes watering as he looked over at his mother. The hard rubber dildo burned in his rectum. Like it was on fire. Ida took another drag, flicked her ashes, and stared.

A pleading look filled Daniel's eyes. Was this good enough? Was he doing what she wanted? Was he a good boy now? Daniel always had the same thoughts when he did this for her. He just wanted it to be over so he could go back to being her little boy again.

Lucinda's thigh was beginning to cramp up from all the thrusting. She took a deep breath, gave a showy moan like she was enjoying herself, and glanced surreptitiously at the clock. She had agreed on half an hour. It would almost be time to renegotiate. She was about to say something when there was a knock on the cab door. Lucinda stopped cold.

Ida shot a look at the door, then got up; she placed her finger to her lips. "You make a sound, I'll beat the both of you." She yanked the curtains closed to the sleeping area.

Outside, Ben waited a moment, then knocked again. The door opened, and Ida looked out. "Yes, Officer?"

Ben peered carefully into the smoky, steamy cab. "Yeah, we have a missing persons report on a seven-year-old girl here, and I wanted to check…."

"Oh, I know. Still haven't found her yet?" Ida asked, trying to sound casual.

"No. Not yet." Ben focused on the curtains that were pulled in front of the sleeping area, "Someone in there?"

Ida glanced over at the curtains, probably a little too quickly, she thought. She looked back at Ben and shrugged it off in her best nonchalant way. "Oh, yeah.

My son. He's asleep. We're a team. Driving keeps us on different schedules." Then she painted on a smile, to sell it. "You know. He sleeps, I drive. I sleep he drives. So on and so on. It's a grind."

"Right. Got it." Ben gave another look around the cab. "What's your name?"

"Ida," the woman answered without hesitation. "Ida Consiglio. My son's Daniel. If we see anything, we'll make sure to report it right away," she offered helpfully.

"Good." Ben was about to turn away when someone rippled the curtains from the other side. His eyes snapped back to the cab. Ida fought the urge to look, too.

"Is he getting up?" Ben asked.

"I, uh, no, he's not due to get up for another few hours. He…." Before Ida could finish, the curtains whipped open.

"It's okay, Momma. I'm up, I'm up."

Ben looked into the bed area. Lucinda was nowhere to be seen; the only hint to her whereabouts was the back window that was slightly ajar.

"You looking for that lost little girl, Officer?" Daniel asked. He was surprisingly good at hiding any hint of what had been going on. He didn't even make eye contact with Ida.

Ben carefully eyed the empty bed area. "Yes, we are."

"Well we ain't seen nothing," Daniel said.

He was starting to sound a bit too smug, Ida thought. Just wait until the goddamn cop was gone and she could lay into him for pulling this bullshit.

Movement out the back window got Ida's attention. She could see Lucinda, sneaking around the side of the truck and running away as she buttoned her top. Ida looked back at Ben, expecting the worst. But he was looking at Daniel. From his angle, he couldn't see what she had just seen.

Ben eased back out the door "All right, then. You make sure you let us know if you do."

Ida leaned forward and grabbed the door. "Yessir, Officer," she said in her best law-abiding voice. "We will. Definitely."

Ben nodded and turned away.

Ida closed the door tight and looked over at Daniel. He could tell by his mother's look that this was going to get very ugly very quickly.

Ten

Ben stood for a moment outside the Consiglios' truck. There was definitely something not right about those two. But then again, there had been no sign of the little girl in their truck, and no other reason to suspect they were up to any kind of kidnapping. Besides, long-distance truckers were always a bit off; it was the kind of job most people couldn't handle. They spent most of their lives in a small cab, driving from one place to the next. If they stopped anywhere too long, they risked losing money for not making the delivery on time. Time and distance were the constant denominator in their lives—the dragon they had to slay. And it was unending. Once a delivery was made, they had to scramble to get another run. Then downtime was the enemy. Their trucks weren't making any money if they weren't delivering something. It was like being in a continual race that you never won. Hurry up and get there. Hurry up and get another job. If they were lucky to have a family somewhere, they couldn't spend too much time with them or they'd be losing out on the money it took to keep a roof over their head. It was what made arrangements like Ida and her son. Better to take your family with you than not see them for weeks on end.

Ben started toward the old Mack truck with the Georgia plates.

* * *

Country music played on the stereo in the dark cab. Inside, the heavyset driver took a sip from a bottle of Old Crow as he stared sadly at a photograph of a nine-year-old girl clipped to the underside of his visor. She was so fresh and open. Her eyes were bright and without any of the suffering he endured. That youth. That energy. He wished there was a way to capture it all somehow. To hold onto it and never let it go. To hold onto *her* and never let her go. It was a deep, primal desire. Not a sexual one. Sex had done nothing but destroy things in his life. It had made him fall into another woman's arms years ago when he was married. Sex had also destroyed the little girl he had loved so much, when she had to go and become a woman.

A beam of light scanned across his pasty face. His watery eyes shifted from the visor to Ben, whom he could see out the window, coming straight for him. He snapped the visor up and stashed his bottle. He struggled as he scooted his big body across the cab and opened the passenger door so he was waiting when Ben approached. "Yes, Officer?" he wheezed.

Ben shone his flashlight into the dark cab. "We're looking for a little girl."

But the driver knew that. How could he forget the slimy young man who had lost sight of his precious daughter? "Yeah," he said. "Her daddy come by earlier lookin' for her."

"Well, we're still looking." Ben's eyes stopped on the full gun rack behind the seats. "Can I see your permits for those?"

The driver looked at the gun rack, then back to Ben "Sure, no problem." He shifted his weight forward, grunted as he leaned over, and opened the glove box. He hated to lean forward like this. It was fucking uncomfortable, and it usually gave him heartburn. "Can't believe he'd leave her alone in a car like that. Oughta have his head examined," he growled, barely able to get the words out. His thick fingers scraped up the permits; he leaned back, caught his breath, and handed them to Ben.

"Thanks," Ben said as he took the permits. "What's your name?"

"Frank Rucka," the big man said.

"You staying here the night?" Ben asked.

"Yeah, figured so, what with the grade closing and all."

Ben perused the permits. A breeze shifted slightly, and he could smell a thick, rancid odor. Ben hesitated and looked up. "What're you hauling back there, Frank?"

Shit. He could smell it. For the first time, Frank seemed anxious. "It's a shipment for Costco."

"Where's your manifest?"

Frank hesitated.

Ben looked more closely at the corpulent, asthmatic man; his intuition kicked in. There was something more going on here. "You have a manifest?"

"Yeah, yeah, of course." Frank reached down between the cab's seats and pulled up a clipboard.

He passed it to Ben, who glanced it over until he found the description of the cargo. "Meat?"

"Yeah."

"Deli meat?"

"Yeah."

"It's a little overdue, isn't it? You were supposed to have it in Phoenix last week."

"Yeah, I was. I just…I had a little trouble."

Ben looked back at Frank, studied him for a moment more, then said, "Show me."

Moments later, Frank unlatched the back door to his truck and pushed it open. The smell hit Ben hard. It cut through even the cold and wet of the Utah night.

"Jesus," Ben coughed. "You have a light back here? Turn on the light."

Frank reached over and snapped a switch. A dim overhead light illuminated the large space. Several pallets of packaged deli meats were stacked in the center. Thick brown puddles of rancid juice surrounded them.

"This is a health hazard, Frank." Ben said. "You know that?"

Frank did know it. He took a moment before answering quietly. "Yeah. I got stuck down south for a few days, and the refrigerator unit burned out."

"And you just left it back there?" Ben said. "What the hell are you planning to do with it?"

"To tell you the truth, I don't know," Frank confessed. "I had a similar problem last month. They said if it happened again, I'd lose my job."

Ben looked over at the depressed, heavyset man and felt sorry for him. He had been right. There was a lot more going on. He handed the manifest back to Frank "Well, my advice is to dump it and let them know. You're putting off the inevitable. If they're going to fire you, they're going to fire you. You're only making things worse for yourself by avoiding it."

"Yeah, I know. You're right. As soon as I can get out of here, I'm gonna bring it on in and face the music."

Ben thought about saying something more, but realized he had probably said enough already. The strangeness out here tonight seemed to be getting stranger. Instead, Ben got back to his business. "If you see anything tonight, you let me know, all right?"

"Of course."

Ben nodded and started away.

Frank closed the back of his truck and watched

Ben leave. He had wanted to tell Ben much more, but he knew he couldn't trust him. He couldn't trust anyone with what was going on with him. It was too dark. Too deep.

* * *

Ben was heading toward the glossy maroon rig when he decided to take a detour. He cut over to Roger's Mustang instead, clicked on his flashlight and shone it around outside. Nothing seemed unusual. The doors were locked. Ben shone the light inside. He could see the blanket in back and the junk food trash on the floor. No sign of the little girl.

Ben stood up and looked over at the diner window. He could see Roger and Kat watching him from inside. He turned and crossed over to the maroon truck. The door opened as he approached.

"That poor little girl still missing, Officer?" the friendly woman in her 60s asked as she peered out the cab door.

"I'm afraid so," Ben answered. "What's your name, ma'am?"

"Florence. Florence White," she answered. "Oh dear Lord. I told him I ain't seen nothing the whole time." Ben looked past her, into the shadowy cab as she prattled on. "You let me know if there's anything I can do, won't you?"

"Just let us know if you see anything." Ben leaned back, his cursory examination of the cab complete, and smiled at the pleasant older woman.

"Yes, yes," Florence said. "Poor thing. Out here in this weather."

Ben had seen enough; she was certainly not someone he should waste any time interrogating. He nodded and started away.

Florence watched him go for a moment, then closed her door. She shifted her angle and could see Ben through her windshield as he crossed over to his patrol car and climbed inside. She watched him click his radio on and start talking to someone as he typed into his squad car computer.

He seemed like such a nice man, Florence thought. It was too bad. He was after all, a man, just like the rest. She knew she couldn't believe all that sweet talk and kindness. In the end they all only wanted one thing, and it was a dirty, unclean thing.

Florence grabbed a pump bottle of hand sterilizer and filled her palm with the cleansing liquid. She rubbed her pale palms vigorously as she watched Ben. She could already imagine what he'd do if he could. His large black hands squeezing her breasts and buttocks like a desperate animal. His lips digging into hers and his tongue ramming down her throat.

God it was hideous. Vile and hideous. And, of course, the worst part of all, the large monstrous thing that would rage from his loins, ripping, stabbing, and violating her.

Florence hated imagining things like this, but she knew she had to. She knew she had to remind herself so she wouldn't be fooled again.

She took a deep breath and looked away from the vile man; the moment was passing, thank God.

She turned and retreated into her sleeping area, her safe place that was filled with glorious little things. Stuffed animals, little jackets, trousers and caps. Her special collection of children's belongings.

Florence settled back and grabbed her collection of little socks, socks that had been on the feet of the little angels. The sweet innocents, pure and unspoiled.

She smiled to herself as she gently caressed the socks. It made her feel so good inside, so calm.

Eleven

All this waiting was driving Roger insane. After he had seen the cop leave Russell's truck, he couldn't believe it. He was seconds away from bolting from the diner and racing over there. If that idiot cop couldn't find Lilly, he could. He would beat the shit out of the degenerate until he confessed.

It was Kat who had talked him down, not with words but by being there. He knew if he had made a move, she would have stopped him. There was something about her that was keeping him grounded.

But now, what was that cop doing in his patrol car? Maybe he had found something and was calling in for more help. Maybe he....

Headlights swung around the side of the building.

Roger looked over. It was a pickup truck. "Now who?" he said.

Kat squinted out the window as the truck came to a stop outside the front door. "It's just Kincaid," she said. "Kincaid Lewis, our mechanic."

The mechanic hopped out of his pickup and hurried inside. He paused in the foyer, stomped the mud off his boots, and brushed the rain off his jacket. "Just got word that the top of the grade's officially snowed closed," he announced.

"Completely?" Kat asked.

"Totally. They're starting to turn traffic away down below, off I-15."

"You leaving?" Kat asked.

"No point in staying."

Bart came out of the kitchen carrying several

boxes of day-old pies. "Got a couple of apples tonight," he said to the mechanic. "I think there's a pumpkin here, too."

"Thanks," Kincaid said as he took the pies from Bart.

Kat glanced back out at Kincaid's truck. She could see someone in the passenger side. "You got company tonight?"

Kincaid looked out at his truck as the person in the passenger side lit up a cigarette. The glow from the flame illuminated Lucinda's face.

Kincaid grew a little embarrassed. "Yeah, well, she needed a ride down the hill. I figured…."

Bart chuckled and slapped Kincaid on the back. "Cold night. Gotta keep warm somehow, right?"

Roger exchanged a look with Kat; this was driving him crazy. The more everyone accepted weird shit like this from these weird people, the more nuts it was making him. He felt like screaming, "Fuck all this. My daughter's missing!"

Kincaid shifted the pies into one arm and took out his keys. He started to turn back to the door, then paused. He looked over at Roger sympathetically. "Hey," he said. "Good luck with everything, huh? Bart's got my number. He can give me a call if you need help with anything. I'm only half an hour down the mountain."

"Thanks," Roger nodded. He put on his most sincere look. It was everything opposite of what he felt.

Kincaid ducked out the front door.

Roger watched as the mechanic climbed into his pickup, started it up, and pulled away. As he was heading out of the parking lot, his headlights swung across Ben, who was coming in from his patrol car. Finally. Fuck, that had taken a long time.

Roger was up and out of the booth when Ben came in. "So? What'd you find out?"

"I've got the Amber Alert for your daughter going out now."

"What about that creep in the tanker truck?"

"I talked to him. At this point, there's no reason to think he's involved. He was just defending his rig. Now if you want to press assault charges...."

"Fuck that. I want to find out what he knows about my daughter," Roger snapped.

Ben raised his hands, trying to diffuse things. "Look, I know he's a bit strange. But I ran his license. Other than a few misdemeanors, he's clean. I've got no reason to bring him in."

"What about the other people out there?"

"I ran their plates. Talked to them too. They might be a little strange, but they're all clean."

Roger slammed his fist on the table. "This is bullshit!"

Ben stood his ground and let Roger simmer for a moment before he continued, calmly. "Roger, I can't arrest people because of how they look."

Ben felt for the hell this man was going through. He knew Roger was feeling utterly helpless and needed to be told what to do with himself during all this, so that's what Ben did. He told Roger exactly what he should do. "You should stay put here until this storm blows over. I'll know where to reach you if I hear anything."

Roger's eyes snapped anxiously back to Ben. "Where are you going?"

"They called me to report down at the bottom of the hill to help close off the highway," Ben said. "As soon as it's secure, I'll come back. I promise."

Roger grimaced anxiously. "Fuck."

Kat looked at Ben reassuringly. "He won't be alone," she told Ben. "Bart and I are here all night."

Bart nodded "We got sleeping rooms and showers if you…"

Roger shot daggers at Bart. "Sleep? I'm not going to fucking sleep!"

Kat gently put her hand on Roger's shoulder. "Then you can stay right out here," she said. "I'll be with you."

There was a moment of silence. Ben assessed the situation, and it seemed to be stable enough for the moment. "All right then. I'll call in as soon as I know anything." He turned and headed out the door.

Roger took a deep, anxious breath. This can't be happening this way. How could there not be a squad of helicopters with searchlights overhead looking for Lilly right now? Where was the team of rescue dogs and volunteers scouring this piece-of-shit truck stop? His entire fucking life was going down the drain, and that cop was being reasonable and logical rather than reacting the way he should. Everyone seemed to be doing everything they could to keep him calm when they should be as freaked out as he was feeling. A storm? An Amber Alert? What the hell kind of bullshit was that to keep them from lighting this whole place up and calling out the National Guard?

Roger felt dizzy; he steadied himself on the edge of the table.

"Roger?" Kat saw him sway unsteadily.

Roger looked away from her and slumped back down into the booth.

There was a moment of silence. They all felt the helplessness Roger was feeling.

Bart looked over at Kat and spoke quietly. "Anything he needs, just go ahead."

Kat nodded. "Thanks, Bart."

Bart headed back into the kitchen.

Roger ran his hands back through his hair and looked out the window. He could see Ben's patrol car pull out of the parking lot, head out onto the highway, and disappear into the misty darkness.

Twelve

A bitter cold breeze swirled through the truck stop complex. The rain had let up for the moment. It had been over an hour since Ben had left, and an eerie emptiness had settled in. No one had come or gone. It was just the four trucks and Roger's car in the parking lot.

But Cedar Mountain Truck Stop was never silent. It was always restless.

Inside the shadowy truck wash, the rows of hanging shammies swayed slightly in the breeze that whistled down the large tunnel.

In the repair garage, the eerie maze of parts and equipment stood silent, but the wind seeped in through the cracks in the sheet-metal siding, causing the chains from the massive engine hoist to tinkle slightly. Kincaid's weird sculpture waited, half-formed, for its artist to return.

And in the back hallway of the diner, there was the lonely dripping sound of the rainwater in the buckets and the rustle of the missing-persons fliers on the bulletin board.

Cedar Mountain Truck Stop was alive and breathing, and it would never rest peacefully. Too many dark and evil events had happened here over the years, and time alone wasn't enough to separate those events from this world.

The only refuge for the living at the moment was inside the warm diner. Bart was busy cleaning the grill in the kitchen, and Kat was at the cash register with Ida and Daniel Consiglio, who had come in to take showers.

"There you go," Kat said as she handed Ida some change. "Towels are in the rooms. Leave them in there when you're done," Kat took out two keys with numbers stamped into them. "Number 5 and Number 6," she said.

"Thank you," Ida said as she took the keys and turned to her son with a stern look. "Daniel." It was a command.

Daniel obediently followed his mother as she started toward the back hallway.

Kat came around the end of the counter and joined Roger, who was still slumped in the booth, staring out the window. He didn't look up. He kept staring out into the darkness. Kat waited a moment, then asked, "Coffee?"

"Can't afford the caffeine," Roger said, still looking away.

"Decaf?"

"Still has some."

"Barely," she said, then grew puzzled. "What's the deal with caffeine? You came in here to buy that energy drink earlier, and that's loaded with the stuff."

Roger grew a bit irritated. "It makes me more aware, that's all. More sensitive, you know, to the things I see."

"Oh," Kat said; it all made sense to her now. She looked over at Bart, busy in the kitchen, then took a seat at the booth.

Roger felt her scooting in across from him; he was being rude and angry, and it wasn't fair to her. She was only trying to help. He turned and looked at her. "Thanks anyway, though."

"No problem. Let me know if there's anything else I can get you, huh?"

"Yeah." Roger mumbled, then looked back out

the dark window.

There was a moment of silence. Kat was torn about what she should say. Nothing seemed right anymore. Anything she could come up with seemed stupid and superficial.

It was Roger who finally spoke, quietly. "I never should've left her out there." His words were full of pain. It was a tortured, horrible thing to confess, and he couldn't even look at her when he said it.

"Roger, it wasn't unsafe. You parked right out there in plain sight. If anyone should feel shitty about all this, it's me. I didn't see her get out."

"You were doing me a favor," he said. "Lilly's my responsibility, and I've been fucking that up for years on my own, trust me."

Kat reached out and gently put her hand on his arm. "Don't do this, Roger."

"No, fuck it. It's true. Most of the time I'm out playing some shitty gig someplace when I should be home with her."

"But you said you're going to stay in Las Vegas from now on."

"Yeah, now. But that doesn't fix what I fucked up before, believe me."

There was another long moment of silence. Kat looked at the tortured man as he continued to stare out into the blackness. He was open and honest with her. No one had been honest with her before, and she felt like she could tell him anything. "You want her. That counts for a lot. My mom ditched me for fourteen years. Then she found me here two years ago. Came in here like nothing ever happened. Bart gave her a job waitressing. We actually got along at first. I started thinking things were going to work out." Kat reached down to a bracelet on her wrist. It was a unique piece of jewelry—woven strands of silver with delicate jade inlays. "We got each other these matching bracelets. We were like regular BFFs. Only then she did it again—took off with some trucker. Haven't heard from her in two years. Nothing. No phone calls. E-mail. Nothing."

"That's fucked up."

"Yeah, but my dad is still around, and that makes all the difference. Like I said, your daughter is lucky to have you."

Roger took a moment to consider Kat's story; she was speaking as someone who had survived a self-destructive parent, and he believed her. Zoe had been deep into drugs from the moment Lilly was born, and even with all his out-of-town gigs and tours, Roger had always made sure he let Lilly know how much he loved her.

A faint flicker of lightning danced in the turbulent sky in the distance followed by a low peal of thunder that rattled the window. Another storm front was on the way. They both regarded it silently; any other time, they would have said something, but after a night like this, it hardly seemed noteworthy.

Kat looked down at the damp stains on the table from Roger's wet jacket sleeve. His clothes were soaked all the way through. She could only imagine how cold he must feel.

She gave him a smile. "So what am I going to have to do to get you to take a hot shower and get into some dry clothes?"

* * *

Roger trudged down the dark, deserted back hallway with a shower room key and some dry clothes from his car. He hadn't cared what he was wearing, but he agreed to shower and change. Anyway, maybe Kat was right. It wouldn't hurt for him to be warm and dry.

Roger approached the bulletin board filled with the missing-persons fliers, and his pace slowed. The collage of eerie pictures took on a new meaning to him now as they fluttered slightly in the strange hallway breeze. His eyes wandered over the yellowing photos of the forever lost, and a dark thought began to cloud his mind. It wasn't the haunted feeling he had had before. It was worse. Much worse. Would Lilly's picture soon be there, too?

Roger looked away, shaking off the horrific idea. No. He would find her. Some way, somehow he would find her.

A low metallic bang came from a side door; Roger shot a look in its direction. It had yellow peeling paint and a faded sign that read "Waste."

Roger hesitated, listened longer. Then it happened again. A low, metallic bang came from beyond the door.

Roger crossed to the door, turned the old knob, and gave a push. It was stuck. He leaned into it with his shoulder and it clunked open. Roger shoved hard and the door swung wide. The loading dock and garbage Dumpsters were on the other side. Roger heard the rapid retreat of footsteps and looked over to see someone disappear around the corner. Who the fuck was that?

Roger darted outside, jumped off the loading dock, and raced around the corner. He looked out across the dark parking lot and saw the favorite-aunt woman struggling with a heavy plastic garbage bag as she climbed into her truck.

Roger stood his ground, considering the older woman's odd behavior. He turned back and crossed over to the Dumpster. He carefully lifted the lid and peered inside.

There was nothing unusual, just the typical garbage that might be found coming from a truck stop like this. Roger let the lid go and it slammed shut. A Dumpster diver. He never would've pegged the friendly woman for a Dumpster diver.

Roger stepped back into the hallway and closed the door. He continued down the hall to the shower rooms, consulted the key Kat had given him. It was room 2. He found the matching door and slid the key in the lock.

A low murmured voice drifted to him in the quiet.

Roger hesitated, turned back. He listened carefully. It was a man's voice coming from inside room 5. Roger crossed over to the other door and pressed his ear to the door.

He could hear water running inside and the muffled voice became clear. It was Daniel whimpering painfully. "Don't make me do it again, Momma. Please don't make me do it again. It hurts."

Roger withdrew from the door, considered the creepy implications of what Daniel was saying. He had decided long ago that the truckers here were strange, but the past few minutes had raised even stranger questions.

Thirteen

Roger went back to room 2, put the key in the lock, gave it a twist, and stepped inside. It was what he had expected. Run down like the rest of the truck stop, but basically clean and in working order.

Roger stripped down, climbed into the shower stall, and pulled the frosted plastic curtain closed.

He stood back from the showerhead and turned on the old spigots. The water pipes groaned and vibrated as the water shuddered on. He adjusted the temperature and the flow and ducked his head under the stream. He grabbed the small paper-wrapped bar of soap from the dish, tore it open, dropped the wrapper on the ledge, and started scrubbing himself.

He looked over at the small courtesy shampoo, considered using it, and decided it was a waste of time. He lathered his hands and scrubbed his hair with the soap.

He stood for a moment under the spray, rinsing his hair clean and letting the hot water wash over him. A moment passed, then another.

Then something dark appeared on the other side of the plastic curtain.

It gathered shape as it moved toward the curtain, stopping right on the other side. It was the shape of a human silhouette.

Roger remained under the stream of water with his eyes closed, unaware as the silhouette raised its hand and began to press inward against the plastic from the other side. The hand grew closer and closer, inch by inch, until the cold touch pressed against Roger's bare back.

Roger spun around, startled, but the silhouette was gone. He peeled the curtain open a crack and squinted out into the bathroom. There was nothing there. No one.

Roger shut off the water and climbed out of the stall. He grabbed the towel, shook it through his hair, dragged it across his face. He looked up at the mirror and stopped cold. Written with a finger in the steamy glass on the mirror were the words, "Find Us."

Roger stared at the message in the eerie silence for a moment, then reached up. With his hand, he wiped the words away.

A loud clunk shattered the silence as the bathroom door closed behind him. Roger spun around. The sound of footsteps retreated outside.

Roger yanked on his pants, pulled on his shirt, slipped into his shoes, and opened the door. He stepped out into the long, dark hallway.

It was empty. The mother and son from the cream-colored truck were gone from the shower rooms next door.

Roger paused and listened. After a moment, the faint sound of someone sobbing came from inside a nearby sleeping room. Roger stepped over to the door and heard his feet splash into something. He looked down and saw a puddle of blood, ebbing out from under the door. Roger grabbed the knob and shoved the door open.

It was too dark inside the sleeping room to see anything at first. Roger waited until his eyes adjusted, then he saw something in the far corner. It was moving. He stepped into the room. It was the covers on the cot. Someone was underneath, sobbing in agony.

Roger's heart thundered in his chest; he swallowed dryly. "Lilly?"

There was no answer. Just the anguished sobbing.

Roger stepped closer, and he could see more. The covers were soaked in blood. Panic surged through Roger; he reached down and yanked back the covers.

But there was no one there. The blood was gone, too.

Wham! The door behind him banged all the way open against the outside wall. Footsteps rapidly retreated.

Roger darted out into the hall in time to see the door with the small window at the far end fly open all on its own. Rain was pouring again outside.

Roger raced down the hall and peered out the open door into the dark downpour. Off in the distance, in the cluttered junkyard, he saw the pale form of a woman standing nude with her arms outstretched, streaked in blood.

Roger hurried out the back door. He pulled aside the broken cyclone fence and stepped into the junkyard. It was a shadowy maze of discarded truck and car parts, tires, mattresses, and old appliances.

Roger scrambled across the soaking debris and reached the spot where he had seen the woman. But there was no one there.

Roger took a moment to catch his breath. He spun around, scanning the junkyard desperately, then yelled out, "Who are you?!"

Strange, static music began to waft out eerily over the junkyard above the drumming rain. At first, Roger couldn't place it, but then it became clearer. It was from the '90s. Joan Osborne. He scanned the clutter and focused in on the source of the music. It was coming from beyond a mound of junk behind an old shed.

Roger started climbing toward the source of the sound. He passed the old shed, traversed a stack of slippery tin siding panels, and clambered down on the other side of the mound of junk. He picked his way over a pile of rotting wood planks halfway submerged in the mud and found the source of the eerie music. It was coming from an old, rusted-out truck cab. Roger stepped closer, wiped the rain from his eyes, and squinted into the empty cab. The music was coming from the dead radio.

Roger stared into the dark cab, then whispered intensely, "What is it? What do you want?"

The radio fell silent. Roger waited for something more. There was nothing but the sound of the incessant rain drumming on the rusted truck roof.

Roger stood up and looked around, his frustrations growing. He sighed anxiously, took a step to leave, and crack! The rotting wood planks in the mud beneath his feet gave way.

Roger plunged downward into the darkness and landed with a splash. He was up to his waist in muddy water at the bottom of a pit that had been opened by the rain, its edges eroded by the water. Roger scrambled to his feet, disoriented. He looked around for a way out, and that's when he saw them. The rotting, dismembered remains of three corpses were moving toward him out of the oozing muck.

Roger cried out, horrified. He shoved the decaying remains away from him and clawed desperately to get out. But the walls of the pit gave way in his hands, and he slipped backward. There was a sickening crack as he collapsed against a woman's upper torso; her ribs sunk into her spine and her head separated from her shoulders.

Roger frantically shoved his way out of the remains and started scrambling desperately up the muddy wall. His fingers dug deep into the soft earth;

he kicked with all his might and sunk his toes into the oozing side of the pit. He pulled himself up, kicked again, and sunk his other foot into the mud. He yanked his hand out and stabbed it into the muck higher up the wall, getting a grip. He reached the top and pulled himself out.

Roger collapsed onto the edge of the burial pit, gasping for air. The rain washed over him, streaking the mud that now covered him from head to foot. He had found something worse than hell. A mass grave of dismembered bodies, buried here by someone who had butchered them in a heinous way.

Roger rallied his strength and rolled over onto his side. He started to pull himself to his feet, but then stopped cold. A small stuffed paw was sticking out from under one of the muddy wood planks at the edge of the pit.

Roger reached over, pulled on the paw and withdrew the lower half of a mud-covered stuffed animal. He carefully scrutinized the shredded remains, and a dark feeling of dread began to overtake him. The color. The fur. The shape.

Lilly's stuffed rabbit. Jimmie Jerry.

"Oh, God. No."

Roger's entire world began to collapse around him. His body went numb. He couldn't feel his grip on the rabbit. He couldn't feel the rainwater streaming over him, or the bitter cold. He tried to inhale, but he couldn't. It was like someone had hit him in the chest with a sledgehammer. The silent moment of horror felt like an eternity. Every emotion Roger had ever felt in his life closed in on itself, imploding in a debilitating black hole.

Then the frozen moment began to thaw. The sounds of the rain returned. The icy cold wetness stung his bare hands. The deep ache in his muscles came flooding back.

Roger staggered to his feet, clutching the stuffed animal's remains. He desperately peered across the dark junkyard. He could see Kat in the diner through the side window.

Roger opened his mouth to yell, but before he could utter a sound, a blinding white beam of light swung toward him from the other side of the junkyard.

Roger spun around. A shadowy figure brandishing a shotgun was coming right toward him. The glint off of a brutally large hunting knife in his other hand flashed menacingly. This was no ghost. This was the killer, and Roger had discovered where he dumped the remains of his victims.

Roger ducked behind the rusted truck cab. The killer snapped off his flashlight and disappeared into the shadowy darkness of the cluttered yard.

Roger peered out from the cab and carefully scanned the area between him and the back entrance to the truck stop. He charted a course in his head that would take him to the break in the fence.

Lightning flickered overhead. The rain started pouring harder.

Roger steeled himself, then got up. He crept carefully around the edge of the burial pit, leaned his weight onto the stack of sheet-metal siding to avoid any unnecessary noise, and pulled himself up. He moved slowly over the slippery sheet metal to the other side and looked back in the direction he had last seen the menacing figure. The pouring rain made it hard to see much of anything. Whoever it was could be anywhere.

Roger looked back toward the truck stop. The break in the fence was in sight. He continued toward the edge of the yard, and another flash of lightning lit up the sky. The killer's silhouette stood three yards in front of him.

BOOM! The dark figure fired wildly at Roger. Roger took a dive.

Inside the diner, Kat heard the gunshot. She hurried to the side window and peered out. Bart ran up behind her. "What the hell was that?"

Outside, Roger scrambled desperately through the tangle of junk; the dark figure zeroed in on the sound of Roger's retreat and took off after him. Roger grabbed a twisted piece of metal from an old motorcycle frame and ducked behind the shed.

He pressed himself up against the corrugated metal wall and raised his makeshift weapon. He listened intently for the sound of the killer's approaching footsteps, but it was hard to hear anything over the pouring rain. He would have to hope for the best and swing when the killer was in sight.

A few seconds passed. Nothing. No one came. Roger began to lose his nerve. The killer wasn't that far behind him. Had he cut around in another direction?

Roger slid to the other end of the shed wall and peered around. Headlights swept across the junkyard. A car was approaching.

It was Ben's highway patrol cruiser.

Fourteen

Ben pulled to a stop in the side lot outside the junkyard; his eyes were fixed intently on the dark, shadowy maze beyond the cyclone fence. Despite the rain, his cop's ears had heard the gunshot when he arrived moments ago, and he could tell the direction it had come from.

He unsnapped his holster, grabbed his flashlight, and opened his door. He was in full cop mode now, careful and alert. He had been trained that way. Safety first. Even when it seemed like a routine traffic stop, treat it like the person behind the wheel could be deadly. And this was even more uncertain. There had been a gunshot.

Ben snapped on his flashlight and shone it across the junkyard. The rain had eased up a bit, and he could see more than he thought he would be able to. But what he saw wasn't helpful; it was just a terrain of tangled clutter.

Ben considered his next move. He was certain it had been a gunshot. He had heard enough of them to know, and this had been a shotgun. But so far there was no one out in the junkyard that he could see.

The back door of the truck stop squeaked open. Ben looked over and saw Bart leaning outside. "Officer? I think we just heard a…."

"Yeah, I heard it too when I was pulling up. Everyone okay inside?"

"Yeah, we're okay," Bart answered.

"Go back inside," Ben ordered. "Lock that door behind you."

Bart retreated into the truck stop and closed the

door tightly behind him.

Ben looked back at the junkyard. It was worth a look. He carefully crossed over to the break in the fence and ducked through. He made his way past the old shed, careful to keep his pistol poised and ready as he panned his light ahead of him through the maze of junk.

He climbed over the mound of slippery metal siding and down the other side to the rusted truck cab and the edge of the dark burial pit. He paused, puzzled. What the hell was this, a collapsed well of some kind?

Ben tilted his light down into the muddy hole. The cold white light landed on the decomposed human remains that bobbed up and down in the murky water at the bottom.

A wave of nausea swept over Ben. "Oh, Christ...."

"Hey!" Roger's voice called out from the darkness.

Ben whipped his flashlight in Roger's direction and aimed his pistol. "Freeze!"

It only took a split second for Ben to see it was Roger, clambering desperately toward him through the junk.

Jesus Christ, Ben thought. You never approach an armed officer like that in the dark. Especially one who had seen what he had just seen.

But Roger wasn't thinking straight. He was panicked and frightened. "He's out here! He was just out here!"

Ben lowered his pistol. "What's going on?"

Roger paused on the other side of the sheet metal pile and caught his breath. "The guy who buried the bodies down there...he saw that I found them...he...he took a shot at me."

"All right, slow down," Ben said. "What guy?"

"I…I don't know, I couldn't see his…."

BOOM!

Inside the diner, Kat screamed as she watched a slug slam into Ben's chest.

"Moth…er…fuck…er," Bart whispered beside her, horrified.

Ben reeled for a split second, clutching the gaping bloody wound in his chest, then pitched backward, crashing onto the metal siding.

Roger took a dive to safety behind a pile of tires. Shit! Had that really just happened? Roger was in raw survival mode now; his body was reacting before his mind could come to terms with the horrific turn this nightmare had taken. He pressed back into the shadows, peered out, and saw Ben was lying dead in a pool of blood.

It did. It had happened. The cop was dead.

Footsteps could be heard retreating. Roger looked around the other side of the tires, but he couldn't see anyone. Then the sound of a truck starting came from the front parking lot.

Headlight beams pierced the darkness, and Russell's old tanker truck swung into view around the side of the building and headed off for the highway. The motherfucker was getting away.

Roger leaped out of hiding in a blind adrenaline rage and clambered across the junkyard to the opening in the fence. He ducked out and cut around the side of the building as the old tanker truck rumbled off down the dark road.

Roger darted to his Mustang, jumped behind the wheel. He fired it up and jammed the gas. The muscle car squealed out of the parking lot.

* * *

The tanker truck threaded its way down the twisting mountain highway. The road was narrow and treacherous in the driving rain and sleet; the old truck's wheels slipped and shuddered when they hit the patches of black ice that had started to form along the edges of the hairpin corners.

Roger could see the taillights of the old truck weaving in and out of view as it went through the turns in the road ahead of him. He gripped the steering wheel of his Mustang with white knuckles; he could feel the slick road under his car as he accelerated. The tattered windshield wipers, their padding long gone in Roger's desperate flight from the parking lot, raced back and forth, doing their best to stem the icy onslaught.

He rounded a corner and saw his opportunity, a straight stretch of road ahead.

Roger jammed on the gas and roared up behind the truck. He cut the wheel hard left as he closed the distance; the Mustang slewed wildly out alongside the truck. Through the dark, vibrating side window of the old tanker, Roger could see Russell's hazy image shoot a look at him. Then the tanker swerved to the left, slamming into the Mustang in a shower of sparks.

"Motherfucker!" Roger yanked his foot off the gas and grimaced as the Mustang careened out of control on the icy wet road, the front end whipping wildly back and forth. He kept turning into the direction of the skid until he regained control.

The son of a bitch had just tried to kill him.

Up ahead, the tanker-truck barreled around a tight corner; the massive wheels rimmed the edge of the road and slammed through a pothole in a shower of icy mud. The brake lights flashed as it was forced to slow.

Roger swerved back onto the road, more determined than ever not to let the monster get away. He jammed on the gas; the Mustang roared and shot forward again. Roger's plan was wild and reckless; he would force the tanker off the road no matter what it took.

The truck crested a rise in the road with the Mustang behind it. Roger leaned forward into the wheel, squinting out of the blurry windshield. He was starting to close the gap between them again when the truck slammed on its brakes.

Roger instantly hit his brakes too, and he saw what the truck was braking for.

A churning flash flood raged across the highway at the bottom on the other side of the rise.

Roger cut the wheel to the right, and the Mustang skidded to a stop on the muddy shoulder.

But the truck couldn't brake fast enough. The back end of the massive tanker shuddered and swung around sideways.

Roger watched, horrified, as the out-of-control big rig careened sidelong toward a massive power line tower on the side of the highway. Roger jammed the Mustang into reverse trying to get away from the inevitable fireworks, but it was too late. The tanker slammed into the tower; the steel latticework buckled instantly and came crashing down on the tanker. The high-voltage power lines snapped and popped and danced wildly in a shower of sparks.

Roger threw open the Mustang door and raced over to the wreckage on the edge of the raging flash flood. A thick sludge was gushing out of a jagged hole in the tanker. It was probably some sort of toxic waste, which would be dangerous but not, Roger hoped, flammable.

Roger carefully threaded his way through the sputtering power lines to the cab of the truck. Russell was slumped over the wheel, unconscious.

Roger yanked open the cab door, grabbed Russell, and shook him violently. "What the fuck did you do with my daughter?" he shouted.

Russell mumbled incoherently, blood streaming down his face.

Roger shook him again. "Where's my daughter?"

Russell drifted off, unconscious.

Roger considered his options; the toxic sludge was swirling up around his feet. The sparking power lines were smoldering and shorting all around him. He had to get out of here. Fast.

Roger grabbed Russell and dragged him out of the truck.

Fifteen

Bart was out in the junkyard covering Ben's body with a plastic tarp when the entire complex was plunged into darkness. He returned to the diner and joined Kat, who was panicking.

Nothing worked. Not even Kat's cell phone. Whatever tower had gone down must have had cell transponders on it.

They looked out the dark window and saw Florence White and Ida Consiglio outside Florence's truck.

"The CB radios in those trucks will still work," Bart said, as he grabbed a couple flashlights from the kitchen. "Here." He handed Kat her own flashlight, and they went outside.

Kat clung to her flashlight tightly, warily scanning the dark parking lot as they made their way toward the women.

"The cell phone relays and the landlines are down," Bart said to the women truckers. "We need to get the police up here. Either of you tried calling out on CB?"

"I got word out about the shooting, but I haven't heard back whether or not the message was passed on to the police," Florence said. "I'm sure it will get to them eventually."

"Well, I got on mine as soon as I saw that murderin' creep drive his rig out of here," Ida said. "But I heard the entire road below here was washed out by a flash flood. Cops ain't gettin' here even if they wanted to."

Kat anxiously peered around the parking lot.

"What do we do?"

Ida gave her a grim smile. "Nothin' we can do, honey. Just tighten your pucker and stay put. Or, you can come on by my rig and have a stiff one with me and my boy."

There was no chance in hell Kat was going to take the leathery old woman up on an offer like that. She didn't even bother to respond.

"We're going to wait it out in the diner. You're all welcome to join us," Bart offered.

"I'll be just fine out here," Florence said with a gentle, motherly smile. Then she pulled out a small, silver, .38 pistol. "If that shooter comes back, he'll have to tangle with me."

At one time, Kat would have been thrown by the sight of the sweet older woman with the pistol, but in the three years she had worked at the truck stop she had come to expect just about anything from the drivers.

They were a tough, self-reliant group, and this was a rough world. Chances are they'd seen shootings like this before. Self-defense wasn't just some kind of "what if" scenario for them. It was part of their daily concern, and most of them could tell you a dozen or more stories about having to threaten the use some kind of lethal force to get out of a jam.

Bart, of course, didn't bat an eye either when he saw Florence's gun. "All right," he said. "But if you change your mind, come on in."

Florence retreated back into her truck. Ida headed back to hers.

As Bart and Kat started toward Frank Rucka's rig, Kat's racing mind returned to Roger. She had seen him take off recklessly after the truck. She knew how desperate he was. "Maybe we should go down and find out what happened to Roger," she said to Bart. "If the road was washed out like Ida said, he couldn't have gotten far."

But Bart shook his head. "We're not going anywhere. No point in that. Not with all that happened here."

Kat started to object but stopped herself. As much as she worried about Roger, she knew Bart was right. She had just seen a policeman gunned down in front of her eyes, and with that, the night had turned deadly. They were all in survival mode now.

* * *

Frank was behind the wheel of his truck, staring at the picture of the little girl on his visor. His eyes were rimmed in red. He was utterly lost and desperate. Everything seemed to have to come to an end for him here. His truck. The spoiled shipment. And the feelings he had been running from for the past three years. He was in a dark corner, and there was no way out.

The .44-magnum pistol in his lap had been there long enough for the cold steel to warm to his body temperature. He looked down at the weapon distantly. It wasn't good or bad. It didn't care. It wouldn't do anything he didn't make it do. It was him. Frank Rucka. He had to do it all, and he was ready.

His hand felt heavy as he reached for the pistol. Then Bart's and Kat's muffled voices from outside shattered the moment.

Frank looked out and saw them approach. He closed his eyes and took a deep breath. Sure enough, they knocked on the door.

"Yeah!" he heard himself call out.

"You okay in there?" Bart's voice was muffled

through the door.

Frank remained motionless with his eyes closed. Go away. Just go away. "I'm fine," he called.

"Well, if you wanna join us inside, you're welcome," Bart offered.

Go inside? With you? Why? To sit around a coffee shop and have to endure the anxious fear of people who wanted to live? Worry about a cop killer who might come back and kill them?

It became clear in Frank's mind. He wasn't trapped. They were. They were trapped because they were trying to hold on to something that they had no control over. They so desperately wanted to stay alive that it tortured them. But not him. Not Frank. He didn't care about his weight, or his diabetes, or his asthma anymore. He was free. He had let go.

"I'm staying where I am," Frank said. And he meant it. This was it. He wasn't going anywhere else ever again.

"Suit yourself," Bart's muffled voice returned. Frank heard their footsteps retreat, and he opened his eyes again. It was black outside. No parking lot lights anymore. Just deep, eternal blackness.

* * *

Bart and Kat headed back toward the diner. Kat took an unsteady breath and shook her head. "Jesus, this is so fucked up."

That was all she could come up with. She had turned things over and over in her mind, trying to find a way to make sense of everything, and she couldn't. The evening had started as a nightmare with Roger's missing daughter and had descended into hell. She felt desperate and helpless and now trapped.

Bart knew she was looking to him to make sense of what had happened, but that would be impossible. The best he could do for her was to remain calm and rational. "We'll be okay. The storm will blow past, and then the cops will...."

Headlights roared up the dark highway. They both looked over and saw Roger's Mustang careen into the parking lot and screech to a stop.

"It's him!" Kat blurted and took off running. Bart followed her. They reached the Mustang as Roger climbed out.

"You're okay," Kat panted, relieved.

Roger shot a stony look back at her and opened the passenger side door. Russell was inside, wounded and groggy.

"What the hell are you doing?" Bart asked, stunned by the sight of the bloodied man.

"Finding my daughter," Roger answered simply as he grabbed Russell and shook him violently. "Wake up! Wake up, motherfucker!"

Bart stepped in and pulled Roger off of the injured man. "Easy! Take it easy!"

Roger yanked his arm out of Bart's grip. "Fuck that. The only reason I didn't kill him down on the highway was so I could patch him up long enough to get answers."

Bart carefully propped Russell's head up and examined his beaten body. "Well, you're lucky you got him this far. He's losing a lot of blood. Let's get him inside, or you're not going to get any answers."

* * *

Moments later, Kat swept a tabletop clean and Bart and Roger laid Russell out on it. Bart wiped the blood that oozed from a cut on Russell's forehead and turned to Kat. "Get the first-aid kit from the kitchen."

Kat hurried off to get the kit. Bart grabbed a stack of napkins from a dispenser and pressed them against Russell's head wound.

"All right, we do whatever we have to do to get this motherfucker awake enough to talk. Don't give him anything for pain. I want him to feel everything," Roger insisted.

Kat returned with the first-aid kit and put it down on the table. Bart tossed the bloody napkins away and rummaged through the kit. "What makes you think it was him?" Bart asked.

"What?" Roger asked, distracted.

Bart found some tape and gauze. "You saw him shoot that patrolman?"

"Well, of course," Roger said irritably. "I heard him run to this truck, then I saw him get in and take off."

"Him? Russell? You saw Russell shoot him? Or you heard it?" Bart asked as he placed the gauze on the wound and pulled off some tape.

"Saw? Heard? Fuck, he was out there running away. He tried to drive me off the road when I came after him," Roger shot back, growing annoyed with the older man.

Bart remained silent as he quietly placed the tape over the gauze, holding it in place.

Roger pressed his point. "Look, you saw what was back there, didn't you? I mean, that pit. The bodies."

"Bodies?" Kat asked, alarmed.

Bart shot a stern look at Roger. Kat was in a fragile enough state; she didn't need anything else on her plate. But Roger ignored him and looked back at

Kat "He didn't tell you?"

Bart looked away angrily and continued to dress Russell's wound. Roger had started something that couldn't be stopped now.

Kat tried to catch Bart's eye but he avoided her. "What's out there?" she said.

"A fucking pit full of remains. Cut up, most of them." Roger said bluntly. He didn't see the point of not letting Kat know exactly what they were all dealing with, especially now that they were isolated like this. Her life depended on it.

Kat went pale. "Jesus. Bart?" She looked desperately at Bart, and this time he couldn't avoid responding.

"Look, you were already so freaked out, I didn't think I should...."

"Bodies? How many?"

"I couldn't tell. I just covered up that officer, and then the power went out, and I came back to you."

"But where did they come from?" Kat asked, reeling.

"This fucker," Roger said, nodding at Russell. "Right here. You said he's been coming around here for years. He's been killing them and dumping them there." Roger took out the muddy stuffed animal remains. "And my daughter's stuffed animal was right out there with them."

"Oh, God," Kat whispered, horrified.

Bart looked over at the stuffed animal that Roger was holding. The depth of rage he was feeling was palpable. Bart struggled silently for a moment, then spoke carefully and measuredly. "Look, we don't know that for sure. We don't know it was Russell."

"He ran. Why would he run?" Roger jumped in.

"You already had him pegged." The last thing

Bart wanted was to get into a fight with Roger now, but he couldn't let this continue to careen out of control. "Hey, I know him. Maybe not well, but I know him. At least fifteen years he's been coming in here. I've got a pretty good nose when it comes to reading people, and he never set off a red flag once. Not once."

"Well, now he has. Especially after what I saw under his truck." The moment Roger said it, he knew he shouldn't have.

"What? What did you see?" Bart grew concerned.

"It looked like he ran over someone." It was the only way Roger could answer without having to explain his visions. The last thing Roger wanted right now was Bart questioning his sanity.

"But the cop checked his whole rig, didn't he?" Bart asked, puzzled. "I saw him do it. If there was something under his truck he would've found it, wouldn't he?"

Roger knew he couldn't say anything else. This was something he had to let go.

"Look, Russell's not going anywhere," Bart said. And he sure isn't going to be talking to anyone soon even if he knows something about your little girl. What we need to do now is chill out until the police get here, and let them deal with this."

Roger sighed, frustrated. As much as he hated to admit it, he knew it was the only logical thing they could do. It didn't matter how much he wanted to beat answers out of Russell, it would have to wait.

Bart looked over at Kat. She could tell by his look that he needed help with Roger. She reached out and gently touched Roger's arm. "Come on," she said.

Roger nodded and turned away with Kat.

Sixteen

It had been at least an hour since Roger had brought Russell back to the truck stop. The rain had let up again, and the temperature had dropped another five degrees. Bart had managed to slow Russell's bleeding and had covered him with a blanket to keep him warm. He stayed by Russell's side, keeping a close eye on the bandages so he could change them when they got too soaked with blood.

Across the diner from Bart and Russell, Roger and Kat sat together at the window booth. Kat had done her best to keep Roger's mind off his daughter. At first, they talked about music. They both had a deep love of many similar bands. And there was definitely a connection between them. If only they had had met at a different time and in a different way, Kat thought. Roger went along with Kat's rather forced conversation for a while, but when he lapsed back into silence, Kat realized it was a futile effort. She asked Roger how he had found the burial pit in the junkyard.

"It was one of them, one of the victims," he said. "She came to me. Led me back there." He looked away, out the window.

"So when you see ghosts like that, they're dying?"

"Dying, just about to die. Whatever the last memory they had here. That's what I see."

"And they can see you and talk to you?"

"And touch me, if I'm not careful."

"But your daughter. You haven't seen her? I mean, as a ghost."

"Doesn't mean anything. I can't control who I see

or when I see them." Roger lapsed back into silence. He looked down at the muddy stuffed animal remains on the table next to him. He felt his throat tighten as his anger rose. "That motherfucker could have killed her, and I wouldn't know it for sure."

Kat studied the tortured man for a moment then asked quietly, "Have you ever tried to contact someone on the other side?"

Roger's expression darkened. After a moment he answered, "Once."

"What happened?"

Roger took a moment before answering. "I crossed over and I almost didn't make it back. One of them tried to hold me there."

"On the other side?" Kat asked.

Roger nodded.

Kat exhaled anxiously. "Jesus."

Roger shifted in his seat. He looked at the clock that had stopped when the power went out. He was growing impatient. "Look, I can't just sit here and do nothing anymore. The bottom line is that Lilly could be dead already, and I just haven't encountered her spirit. As hard as it's gonna be, I need to find out, and there's only one way to do that from this side."

Kat hesitated before asking the question she was afraid to hear the answer to. "How?"

* * *

Moments later, Kat had her answer. They gathered a snow shovel from the janitor's closet and pushed out the back door of the complex. They were headed to the burial pit to search for any more traces of Roger's daughter.

Roger panned his flashlight over to the break in

the fence. "Come on."

They crossed over to the break and ducked through. Roger led the way as they carefully picked their way to the stack of wet tin siding by the old shed.

"It's just on the other side," Roger said as he reached back to help Kat. "Careful. It's slippery."

Kat took his hand, and he helped her up onto the corrugated panels. Her feet slipped a little, but she caught herself and managed to get to the other side.

Roger tucked the flashlight in his front pocket and took a step up onto the siding. He used the shovel to steady himself. A faint, ragged breathing chilled the back of his neck.

"Please, please. No," he heard from behind him.

Roger spun around, slipping off the siding. He looked behind him and saw the shadows of the old shed shift and move. A terrified woman peered out from hiding. She was covered in blood; her late '90s-style dress was ripped apart, and her left arm had been hacked off completely.

She locked eyes with Roger, pleading in a halting voice. "Don't…let him get me…please…he's right there…." She looked desperately behind her at an unseen assailant who was closing in on her.

"Roger?" Kat's voice invaded the moment. Roger looked over at Kat. She aimed her flashlight down at him with a concerned look on her face. "What is it?"

Roger spun back to look at the shed. The mutilated woman was gone.

Roger took a deep breath, closed his eyes. "Shit." He turned back, pushed himself up onto the stack of siding, and carefully crossed over to Kat.

"You going to be okay?" she asked, growing more worried.

"Yeah, I just saw one," Roger answered

unsteadily.

"A ghost?"

Roger nodded. "Yes."

Kat looked back at the old shed, unnerved. "Where?"

"Back there." Roger registered Kat's unease. "It's okay. They're probably everywhere back here. You won't see them. They can't reach you."

"What about you?"

"I'm used to it," he answered, doing his best to convince himself. Then he reached out for her hand. "Come on."

They continued deeper into the junkyard. Roger shone his flashlight through the maze of junk and stopped on the old, rusted-out truck cab. "It's over here."

They passed around the truck cab and reached the edge of the burial pit. Rivulets of water were still streaming down into the gaping hole. Roger passed his flashlight to Kat. "Don't get too close to the edge," he said. "But try to keep the light aimed down there so I can see."

"You're going down in there?" Kat asked, surprised. She didn't remember this being part of the plan. "You said you found Lilly's stuffed animal up here."

"All the bodies are down there, and everything else nearby is washing down in there now anyway," Roger said, as he paused on the muddy edge of the pit and looked down into the darkness.

Kat knew why they had come out here, but now, seeing Roger poised on the edge of the deep pit, it seemed like a terrible idea. "Roger, are you sure you want to do this?"

Roger took a shaky breath. It was the same

question he was asking himself. There was every rational reason not to do this, but this wasn't about anything rational. This was about his daughter and about learning if she was dead or alive. He answered the only way he could. "I've got to know," he said.

He grabbed the edge of the rusted truck cab with one hand and started lowering himself, feet first. "I need more light," he called up to Kat. "Give me more light."

Kat leaned closer to the edge and adjusted the angle of the flashlight beam. The pale light illuminated the bottom. It was filled with murky water now.

Roger let go of the truck cab and held onto the muddy edge with both hands. He let himself slide down slowly, controlling his speed with his tenuous grip in the muddy walls.

He looked over his shoulder beneath him. His feet were just above the water when there was a loud whoosh!

A hand burst out of the murky liquid and grabbed his ankle. Roger recoiled, horrified, as a young woman, covered with blood, pulled herself out of the black water. Her eye sockets were empty holes of bloody flesh, and her jaw had been hacked off on one side so that it drooped open at a hideous angle.

Kat saw Roger frozen above the water. "Are you all right?" she asked.

Roger took a deep breath, closed his eyes, and opened them again. The woman was gone. "Yeah. Yeah, I'm okay."

He lowered himself the rest of the way. The water reached his waist by the time his feet sank into the muddy bottom. He looked back up at Kat. "Give me the shovel."

Kat held the shovel out to him.

"Don't get too close to the edge," Roger reminded her.

She stretched her arm as far as she could, and Roger grabbed the handle at the bottom. "Got it!"

Kat let go of the other end and took an unsteady step back from the muddy ledge.

In the pit, Roger dipped the shovel into the murky depths and started dredging the bottom. He could feel the scoop catch on several solid masses; some were hard, like stone, and the wood handle of the shovel vibrated.

He pulled it upward; the items were heavier than he expected, and he strained in his effort. The dingy water washed away as the scoop broke the surface, revealing a rotted skull and several fingers.

Kat choked back a sickened reaction and looked away.

"The light! Don't move the light!" Roger yelled up at her.

Kat was forced to re-aim the flashlight at the bottom.

Roger carefully examined the old remains in the pale light. The teeth had been pulled from the skull; the tips of the fingers were missing. Roger dumped the remains onto a muddy ledge and went in for another pass with the shovel. This time it hit something even heavier. Roger grimaced, pushed against it; his mind raced at the possibilities of what it might be. A torso? A leg?

"What is it? What's wrong?" Kat called from above.

"Nothing. It's something heavy." Roger bore down with all his might, working the shovel back and forth. Then the shovel slipped off whatever it was under.

Roger crashed back into the muddy wall. The wet, heavy earth gave way.

Kat leaped back as the edge of the pit slid downward. "Roger!" she screamed.

The mudslide oozed into the bottom of the pit, exposing several more dismembered corpses. Roger struggled to avoid the onslaught, but it was no use. It pinned him against the opposite side.

Kat dropped to her knees and reached down. "Take my hand!" she shouted.

Roger shoved the newly exposed rotting body parts out of his way and groped for her hand.

She strained and leaned out as far as she could; they reached each other. Kat leaned back and pulled with all her might.

Roger kicked and struggled to free himself from under the muck. He crawled up the sloped side of the pit on his knees and made it to safety on the edge.

Kat let go, out of breath. "Are you okay?"

"Yeah, I'm fine," Roger coughed as he squinted and wiped the mud off his face.

Kat reached down to pick up her flashlight and stopped cold. A horrified look crossed her face, and she emitted a hoarse whisper. "No...."

Roger looked over at her, puzzled "What's wrong?"

She was staring into the pit; the shocked look frozen on her face.

Roger turned and looked where she was aiming her flashlight. There was a woman's dismembered arm among the newly exposed remains, with a bracelet on its wrist. It was woven strands of silver with delicate jade inlays.

Kat started trembling uncontrollably, and she dropped the flashlight.

"Kat? What is it?"

Kat reached down and touched the identical silver bracelet on her own arm—the twin to the one her mother owned. "It...it's..." she stammered. Tears spilled down her face, her kneels buckled, and she reeled.

Roger caught her before she collapsed. He looked from the bracelet to the one on the dismembered arm, and it all became clear. "Your mother," he whispered.

Seventeen

Russell groaned softly and stirred on the table in the diner. Bart grabbed a glass of water that he had standing by. "Hold on. Here." He cradled Russell's head in his hand and brought the glass of water to his lips.

Russell swallowed dryly, tried to take a sip. The water met his lips and trickled into his mouth. He started to cough and choke.

"All right. Okay, slow. Slow." Bart pulled the glass away until the coughing subsided.

Russell started to shake his head as he tried to focus his bleary eyes on Bart. "Nnn…no, I…I…." he whispered hoarsely.

Bart leaned down close to Russell, trying to hear. "What?"

"It…it…wasn't…." Russell trailed off, growing groggy again.

"Russell?" Bart raised his voice, trying to wake him again but it was no use. Russell was asleep. Bart carefully slid his hand out from under Russell's head and set the glass down. He was considering what to do next when a low thump came from across the dark, shadowy diner. Bart looked over. "Hey guys, get in here. He was starting to talk."

Bart waited for Kat or Roger to answer, but instead there was nothing. "Kat?" he tried again.

There was still no answer.

Bart stood, looked across the diner. A faint yellow glow was emanating from the kitchen. Bart grabbed his flashlight and started toward it.

Kat sobbed uncontrollably in Roger's arms as they made their way to the edge of the junkyard. If he hadn't been there to help her, she would've collapsed.

Everything Kat had ever felt about her mother was racing through her mind at once; her thoughts were scattered and her words couldn't keep up. "This whole time, I…I thought she had left again. I thought she didn't want to see me. I thought…she…" A new wave of tears wracked her body, and she couldn't continue.

Roger pulled her close, doing what he could to comfort her. His mind centered on Russell. They were both victims of that monster in the diner now, and it fueled his rage even more. "I don't give a shit how hurt that motherfucker is. I'll beat him awake. I'll fucking choke him until he tells me where Lilly is, and then I'll kill him for what he did to your mother. I swear I…."

Roger stopped abruptly.

Kat collapsed against him, looked up at him through her tears. She could see a wary expression on his face. "What?" she sniffed, growing frightened.

Roger didn't answer.

Kat looked over in the direction he was staring. The back door to the dark building was banging eerily in the wet breeze.

"Roger? What is it?"

"I closed that door tight when we left."

"What do you think…?"

"Shhh…" he cut her off. They continued up to the swinging door. Roger raised his flashlight and peered inside.

The long, dark hallway was empty.

Roger looked back at Kat, put his finger to his

lips, and stepped inside. Kat clung tightly to his arm.

They crept quietly past the shadowy doors to the sleep rooms and showers, which were all tightly shut. They reached the door to the diner. It was partially open. Roger exchanged a look with Kat, then pushed it further.

Pale smoke hung in the air inside the diner. The faint sound of something frying came from the kitchen. Roger swung his flashlight beam across the dark diner and stopped at the table where they had left Bart and Russell.

There was blood everywhere. Russell's lifeless body lay in a heap on the floor in front of it, his throat slashed open from ear to ear.

Kat stifled a scream. Roger silenced her with a look and moved his light over to the kitchen. A flickering yellow glow played against the walls.

Roger stepped around the counter, reached out, and pushed the kitchen door open.

Bart was slumped face down on the red-hot cooktop, a knife sunk in his back. His face popped and sizzled as it fried against the scalding surface; his shirt smoldered.

Kat screamed.

Roger hurried over, shoved Bart off the cooktop. His lifeless body tumbled back, revealing his bubbling and smoldering face.

Roger choked and coughed on the sickly smoke and shut off the burner. He looked around frantically, grabbed a butcher knife, and held it out to Kat. "Here!"

Kat backed away, trembling, shaking her head. "There's a pistol under the register." She turned and bolted out of the kitchen.

"Kat! Wait!" Roger called after her, but she was gone.

Kat ran into the diner and raced behind the cash register. She reached into the shelf underneath and felt around frantically. "Shit." She looked up at Roger as he hurried in. "It's gone. Roger, it's gone! What do we do?"

Roger rushed over to the front door, twisted the lock shut. He aimed his flashlight at the door to the back hall. "Can you lock that?"

"I think so." Kat grabbed a large ring of keys from a drawer by the register. "It's one of these."

Roger took the keys from her and hurried to the hallway door. He examined the lock, then started trying one key after the next, hoping for a match.

Kat looked across the dark room at Russell's lifeless body, lying in the pool of blood under the table. "We were wrong this whole time. We were wrong about him."

"Yeah, and that means whoever did this is still here." Roger found the right key, twisted it in the lock. He tested the metal door, then backed away, still not satisfied.

He grabbed a nearby chair and wedged it up under the knob. "There." He stood back, caught his breath. "No one's getting in through there without us knowing it."

Roger turned, crossed over to the large front windows. He looked out at the shadowy trucks in the dark parking lot. "Fucking freaks," he said. "It could be any one of them out there. You know I heard that sicko mother and her son together in the shower earlier."

"What?"

"Yeah. Together. Same shower. They were up to some freaky shit. And that other old lady. There's something going on with her too."

"But it could also be someone else, couldn't it?

Someone we don't know," Kat said as she stepped up behind him.

Roger shook his head "I doubt it. Whoever it is knows this place…knows it well…they've been dumping bodies back there for years. Like that fat fuck with all the guns. He's been around."

"So when the police get here, we just…."

"Forget the police. It could be hours before they get here, and those are hours that Lilly might not have. If she's still alive, every second now could mean the difference between life and death for her."

"So what do we do? We can't go after all of them."

Roger stared out at the ominous collection of trucks for a moment in silence, and a dark look crossed his face. "No. We can't go after all of them, but we might not have to." He trailed off; his mind raced as a desperate idea began to form.

Kat saw the look on his face and grew concerned. "What? What is it?"

Roger didn't answer.

"Roger?"

He looked back at her. "I could reach over and find out."

"Reach over? What're you talking about?"

"I could make contact with one of those victims back there in the junkyard. They could tell me who killed them."

"You mean you'd cross over?"

"Yeah, and I could find out who the killer is."

"But you said it almost killed you when you tried it before."

She was right, of course; he had almost died when he had done it before. It had been a reckless thing to try, and he had done it when he was in a particularly reckless state of mind. At the time, he was a sophomore at Davis, and he had tried many self-destructive things in his attempt to drown out the noise and visions that made his life so unbearable.

He had been dating Claire, a twenty-year-old sophomore from San Francisco. They met at a frat party when they were both stoned. After that, most of their dates were spent downing Xanax and Vicodin together. Eventually she had tried to get sober, and she said the only way would be to leave him. Roger had been devastated, but he was used to the instability of life as a victim of his psychic gift, which required him to be a functioning junkie. Roger's solution was the usual numbing of his feelings with his opiates.

Several months later, he heard that Claire had died of an overdose. Even in Roger's heavily medicated state, it cut deep. She had left him to get clean, and she hadn't been able to follow through with it. It was strange, but Roger was jealous of the drugs she had chosen over him; it was as if she had cheated on him. He couldn't help but think that if only she had stayed with him, maybe she wouldn't have overdosed.

Alex, Roger's roommate at the time, had been an animal science major. They had spent long hours together, and Roger had opened up to him about his encounters with the dead. Alex was a believer, and he was endlessly fascinated by it. Roger couldn't remember exactly whose idea it was at first, but once the seed was planted, it grew quickly.

Roger would cross over and seek out Claire. Roger had always known that stimulants seemed to trigger his visions, so this time they would take it a step further and try to force one to occur. Alex managed to get some synthetic adrenaline from the veterinary school, and Roger scored some coke from his Vicodin dealer.

That night they broke into the dorm room where Claire had overdosed. Roger ingested the drugs and slipped over to the other side.

In the years since this had occurred, Roger had forced himself to forget what happened next, and for the most part he had been successful. But the one thing he could never forget was the feeling of Claire's icy, dead touch on the other side. She had held onto him, desperate not to let him return.

Back in the living-world, Alex saw Roger drifting away; his body was shutting down, and he was close to dying. Alex went into a panic. He pounded on Roger's chest to get his heart going again and had all but given up when Roger returned.

The two of them never spoke about what they had done. Of course it was a story they couldn't tell without having to answer too many questions. The next semester, Alex transferred to UCLA, and Roger lost touch with him. Roger went downhill quickly after that. It was the beginning of his big slide into the heavy narcotics that almost took his life.

To Roger, this was now just another chapter in his tortured life. A lesson he had learned. Another nuance in the ways his "gift" could destroy him.

Of course Roger knew the risks he would be taking if he tried this again, but with precious time ticking way that Lilly might not have, it seemed well worth it.

Roger gently put his arm on Kat's shoulder and looked at her reassuringly. "That was something different. I know what to watch out for now. I'll be careful."

But Kat was still dubious and frightened. The one person she could count on now was talking about risking his life.

Roger could see she still wasn't convinced. "Kat, I'm telling you, this could work. Any one of those victims could tell me who the killer is. And if I end up seeing Lilly on the other side too, then at least I'll know." As hard as it was to say, it was the truth. He could find out for sure.

Roger looked away from her. It didn't matter what she said now, he was convinced, and he was going to do it. "I'll need uppers. Uppers and speed. Lots of it, like caffeine, only more, so I can heighten what I feel, heighten my senses."

Eighteen

Roger dumped a six-pack of Red Bull, several Monster Energy drinks, and a couple of packages of NoDoz onto the booth table.

Kat hurried in from the kitchen with a defibrillator kit. "We've had it here for a couple of years. I've never used it."

Roger poured out a handful of NoDoz and washed the pills down with a Red Bull. "Hopefully you won't have to. Just keep an eye on me." He downed more NoDoz, finished off the can of Red Bull, and opened another.

Kat grabbed her purse and dug out a small plastic pouch. "Here. Not much left, but it might help."

Roger took the small pouch and opened it. "Coke?"

"Big party in Salt Lake last week," she said, as she rolled up a dollar bill.

Roger tapped out a line on the table.

Kat gave him the rolled bill, and he snorted up the line. "What else you got?"

"I wish," Kat smiled faintly.

Roger wiped the residual coke off the table, rubbed his gums with it. He cracked open a Monster drink, poured out another handful of NoDoz, and washed them down. He paused, took a sudden deep breath. "Yeah. Yeah, I'm feeling it." Roger pushed the unopened drink cans aside and lay down on his back on the table.

"So I just watch you?" Kat stepped closer, concerned.

"If I stop breathing, zap me." Roger took another

deep breath and started to focus his thoughts on his surroundings. The smell of the burned flesh in the kitchen filled his nose. He could hear the light sound of the rain outside, the low rumble of a truck's generator in the parking lot. He could feel the cool Formica tabletop against his back, and the way the edge of the table cut into the back of his ankles as they extended off the end. He was becoming hyper-aware of everything around him.

Kat watched him breathe deeply in and out for a moment. "Roger?" she asked quietly.

"Yeah?"

"If you see my Mom, tell her I love her."

"I will."

Then it started. Roger's breathing began to speed up involuntarily. He could feel his heart hammering in his chest. Everything around him began to become saturated and vivid. He closed his eyes and sank into the blackness.

* * *

The moment Roger opened his eyes again, he remembered the hollow feeling inside, just as when he had done this before. His impulse to breathe became unnecessary. He could simply exist.

He was standing over himself at the booth. Kat was still at his side, watching him carefully. It was cold and eerie. All the color was gray and monochromatic. The sounds were isolated and dead. It was the inverse of the living-world.

Roger stepped away from himself and crossed the diner, heading for the back wall. His footsteps fell in dull thuds against a floor that felt like it was made of thick clay.

A guttural gagging sound drew his attention to a nearby booth, and he looked over. A middle-aged truck driver, dressed from some time in the late '60s, was on his knees, choking to death on his food. His desperate eyes met Roger's as he convulsed and clutched his throat.

Roger looked the other way, then he stepped right through the back wall and out into the dull, gray parking lot. It wasn't night or day here. It was some time caught in between, a perpetual twilight.

He started down the side of the building and passed a woman from some time in the 1970s. She was sprawled out on the ground, clutching her chest in the throes of a heart attack. She pleaded desperately as Roger passed, "Please… please…hel…help…."

Roger kept moving straight ahead, being careful not to get too close. He rounded the end of the building and came upon a bleeding homeless man.

Roger stopped short, backed away.

The old man groaned in agony as he clutched a knife wound in his gut.

Roger slipped quietly around him, stepped through the broken chain link fence, and entered the junkyard.

A woman's desperate cry for help swirled out of the eerie dead stillness. Roger started toward the sound. This was it. This was who he had come looking for.

As he approached the old shed, the bloody, mutilated woman in the tattered '90s dress staggered into view. She looked behind her, trying to get away from her unseen assailant.

This was Roger's chance. He cut around behind the woman and reached out to her. A jolt of energy surged through Roger's body as he touched her. There was a blinding flash of white light; Roger's entire being vibrated with a jittery charge of adrenaline. Then the whiteness faded, and Roger could see what the woman was seeing through her eyes.

The killer's hand was looming right at him with a large hunting knife. The blade plunged downward. Roger looked down at the woman's body as the blade sunk deep into her stomach. Her scream shattered Roger's ears. He looked back up and saw the killer's face.

It was Kincaid, the truck stop mechanic.

He was twenty years younger but recognizable. There was an anxious, panicked look in his eyes; sweat glistened off his pale face.

Roger yanked his hand off of the woman and staggered back, reeling from the vision. Of course, it all made sense. This was Kincaid's own backyard. He had been working here for at least the last two decades.

Roger backed away from the dying woman; he had to get back to the diner and tell Kat. As he turned to leave, he came face to face with the real, living-world Kincaid.

Roger tried to duck out of his way, but it was too late; he felt a flash of unbearable heat flood his numb body as the living-world Kincaid passed right through him as though he wasn't even there.

Roger staggered back and watched, horrified, as the living-world Kincaid entered the back door of his repair garage.

Roger hurried over and passed through the garage wall in time to see the living-world Kincaid open one of the doors and grab a shotgun from a storage room in back. He crossed over, yanked open a drawer in his workbench, grabbed what looked like janitor's keys, and picked up a fresh box of ammunition. He emptied the box of ammo into his jacket pocket, tossed the carton away, then reached back into his pocket and took out a couple of shells. He started to the door, loading the shotgun as he went.

Roger scrambled out of Kincaid's way as he passed within inches, then hurried out after him. Kincaid racked the shotgun and made a beeline to the back of the truck stop. He was heading to the diner to finish what he started. Kat and Roger would soon be dead like the rest.

Nineteen

Roger took off running as fast as he could to the diner. He had to rejoin his body and get Kat out of there before Kincaid could get to them.

Roger rushed to the side of the building; he was about to pass through the wall to the diner when a bloody hand grabbed him from behind. Roger felt himself tumbling, and he hit the cold, mud-like ground, hard.

He twisted back and saw Ben's spirit, grimacing in agony, bleeding from the shotgun wound in his chest. His highway patrol uniform was soaked in fresh blood. "Don't…don't leave me." The words gurgled from Ben's throat as blood oozed out of his mouth.

Roger desperately kicked and struggled to get free from Ben's spirit, but Ben clung tight to Roger. Fear and confusion filled Ben's eyes; his death was fresh and his spirit was strong. He was much stronger than Claire's spirit had been all those years ago, when Roger had been foolish enough to have crossed over before.

Roger looked over and saw the living-world Kincaid enter the back door of the truck stop. Roger renewed his effort to free himself from Ben, but the spirit held him in an icy death grip, "Help me…don't leave me…."

Back in the living-world inside the diner, Kat could tell something was wrong. Roger's breathing was becoming shallow and slow.

She shook his body. "Roger? Roger!"

But it was no use. Roger's breathing slowed even more. Then she heard footsteps approaching from the other side of the hallway door.

She looked over in a panic. The footsteps stopped outside the door. There was a moment of silence, then the doorknob twisted slowly back and forth.

Kat spun back to Roger and shook him violently. "Roger! Come back! Hurry!"

In the dead-world outside, Ben's spirit held Roger's leg in an icy grip as he pleaded desperately. "Please…take me…take me back with you…."

Roger began to grow weak, unable to fight back against the powerful spirit. His life force was dwindling fast; he could feel the bone-numbing cold creep up from where Ben was holding onto him. Roger knew he was losing his hold on his body in the living-world, but he was powerless to fight it. The icy feeling that was spreading up his legs would soon consume his soul completely.

Back in the diner, Kat frantically opened the defibrillator unit and took out the paddles. The step-by-step instructions were large and illustrated; she read step one and threw the switch. The unit began to warm up.

Across the diner, the door lock sprang open. Kat looked over in a panic. Whump! The door slammed open into the chair that Roger had put under the knob.

Kat screamed, terrified. She ripped open Roger's shirt and grabbed the defib paddles.

Outside in the dead-world, Ben's spirit clawed his way up Roger's leg hand over hand. Roger gasped weakly; the fight had left him. All that was left was to give in and accept his fate. He closed his eyes and felt the icy numbness wash over his torso and spread out to his limbs.

In the diner, Kincaid slammed the door repeatedly against the chair. He moved it several inches. Just enough. His hand groped inside for the chair. If he could shove it out of the way, he could open the door; his fingers managed a tentative purchase on the back of the chair.

The defib unit beeped. It was ready. Kat jammed the paddles into Roger's chest. They zapped loudly. Roger's body jerked spastically, his back arching off the table.

At the same instant in the dead-world, a jolt of energy shot through Roger's soul. His eyes snapped open; he reached down, yanked and kicked hard at the same time, sending Ben's spirit crashing backward. Roger staggered to his feet, backed away from Ben, then turned and stepped through the diner wall.

Back in the living-world, Kincaid gave a final shove on the metal door, and the wood chair shattered to pieces.

Kat dropped the paddles and screamed. Kincaid kicked the door open wide, and at the same instant Roger bolted upright on the table, inhaling sharply.

"Roger!" Kat yelled. He was back and awake. But her relief was short-lived. BOOM! Kincaid took a wild shot as he barged in through the door.

Roger rolled off the table and tackled Kat. Another gunshot echoed through the diner. Buckshot shredded the table above them as they scrambled, on their hands and knees, to the other side of the wait-station.

Kincaid racked the shotgun, strode through the shadowy diner. His expressionless, cold eyes scanned the darkness for them. This was going to be over soon.

Kat and Roger crawled their way quietly under the tables and chairs until they reached the front of the diner. Roger looked back and saw Kincaid's feet pause several yards away.

Roger turned to Kat and whispered, "Follow

me."

"Where?" she whispered back.

"The window." Roger reached over, grabbed a chair leg. He gave Kat one final nod, then leaped up and heaved the chair at the large front window. The chair exploded through the glass.

Kincaid spun around, took aim. Roger and Kat dove out the window as Kincaid fired. The buckshot tore through the remaining glass, just missing Roger and Kat.

They tumbled into the wet parking lot. "Up! Get up!" Roger yelled as he grabbed Kat's shoulder. They took off across the dark lot to Frank Rucka's dilapidated truck. Roger pounded on the cab door desperately. "Hey! Hey, open up!"

"Help us, please!" Kat joined in.

Roger looked back at the diner and saw Kincaid's shadow looming inside the shattered window; he racked the shotgun again.

Roger gave up pounding and tried the door. It was unlocked. He shoved the door open and revealed a horrific sight: Frank's dead body behind the wheel.

He was slumped forward; the back of his head was blown open, his pistol still in his mouth. There was blood everywhere. Tatters of brain and flesh covered the seat behind his head. He had done what he had promised himself he would do. He had left his misery behind.

Roger stared at the sickening sight, stunned "Jesus," he said. Kat recoiled, gagged and wretched.

BOOM! Buckshot shredded the truck next to her.

Roger grabbed her and they took off toward the next truck. Before they could get there, the cream-colored truck rumbled to life. Pop. Hiss. The brakes released.

"What the fuck're they….?

The truck lurched forward and the headlights snapped on. In the pale glow of the cab, they could see Ida behind the wheel with a terrified look on her face. She swung the wheel wide, and the truck pulled away from Roger and Kat, heading for the highway.

"Fucking bitch!" Kat screamed. The truck sprayed them with mud as it roared past.

"Hey!" Kat yelled desperately. But Roger knew it was useless. Ida wasn't about to stop, and they'd need another plan. He looked back across the parking lot. Kincaid was climbing out the broken diner window.

Roger grabbed Kat's hand. "Come on!"

They ducked over to the maroon truck, and Kat pounded on the door. "Florence! Flor…!"

Before she could yell again, the door popped open, revealing the sweet older woman brandishing her pistol with a hardened look on her face. "Get down," she commanded.

Roger and Kat ducked, and Florence opened fire.

Her barrage strafed the diner window across the dark parking lot. Kincaid took a dive back inside the safety of the diner.

Florence emptied her clip, popped it out, jammed in another, and reached down for Kat's hand. "Come on, honey. Inside!"

Kat reached up for the woman's hand, but before she could take it, a shotgun blast rang out from the diner. The heavy slug punched into Florence's chest. The older woman teetered, looked down with a surprised look on her face, then pitched over and tumbled out onto the wet pavement, dead.

Several more rounds exploded from the diner. Roger and Kat ducked. The slugs pummeled the truck cab, shredding the dashboard, which sparked and popped.

Roger looked around desperately. They had no place to run. No more trucks. He looked back at his car, still parked right outside the diner. If they could lure Kincaid away from the diner, maybe they could circle back and get to his car. Roger scanned the parking lot again; his eyes locked on the large, shadowy truck wash.

"Come on!" They took off together across the parking lot.

Twenty

Kat and Roger ducked into the long, cavernous building.

"This way," Roger said.

They darted down the damp tunnel, squeezed past the massive brushes and into the forest of dangling shammies. The damp, cold strands of terry-coated rubber clung to their skin as they pushed their way through and out the other side.

Roger pressed back against the wall and pulled Kat close. They paused for a moment, catching their breath. Roger peered out through a narrow crack between the brushes and the shammies.

He could see Kincaid step out of the diner in the distance. He kept his shotgun poised and ready as he scanned the dark parking lot. After a moment, he lowered the shotgun. It was clear he didn't know where Kat and Roger had gone.

Kat clung tightly to Roger as she whispered, "I can't believe it… Kincaid. Him. He's doing this. What're we going to do now?"

"We can wait until he's away from the diner, then we can circle back and get my car." Roger gingerly touched the red burn marks on his chest from the defibrillator paddles and grimaced.

"Are you all right?"

"Seem to be," Roger nodded.

"What happened? You stopped breathing."

"That cop grabbed me. Didn't want to let go."

"Shit," Kat exhaled.

"But I didn't see Lilly anywhere. She must still be alive."

It was true. He hadn't seen Lilly, and that was a good thing. But Roger was trying to put an optimistic spin on it for Kat. Just because he hadn't seen her didn't mean that she wasn't on the other side someplace. He had only gone to the junkyard, where he knew he would find the victim he had encountered before. He hadn't had the chance to search for Lilly once he had seen the living-world Kincaid heading to the diner to kill them.

But Roger's words did make Kat feel somewhat relieved and she managed a small smile. "Thank God. that's good. That's very good."

Roger peered back out the crack between the shammies and the brushes where he had seen Kincaid seconds before, but this time Kincaid was gone.

"Fuck."

"What?"

"I don't see him." Roger anxiously adjusted his angle, trying to regain sight of Kincaid. It was useless. The parking lot was empty.

"Where the hell did he…?"

Roger gave up; he looked in the other direction, down the long truck wash tunnel. "We should probably keep moving."

He took Kat's hand, and they crept deeper down the tunnel, squeezing around the huge spindles of the secondary brushes. An eerie breeze picked up as they neared the other end of the truck wash. The bristles on the brushes behind them vibrated and rattled.

They stepped into the drying station, filled with hanging terry-cloth strips, and then moved to two massive, side-by-side spring-loaded rubber squeegees.

Roger grabbed the edge of the squeegee and pushed it aside. Kincaid was right there.

Kat screamed and recoiled. Roger let go of the

squeegee, and it snapped back into Kincaid, knocking him off balance. His shotgun blasted wildly.

Roger grabbed Kat. "Here!"

He pulled her over to a side door and shouldered it open.

A gust of icy wind kicked up as they stumbled out of the truck wash. Roger's eyes locked on the nearby repair garage. "Tools," he said. "Tools make good weapons."

They took off toward the garage with the hope of finding a way to defend themselves.

* * *

It was dark and cluttered, and it smelled of rancid engine grease. But there was something else that smelled, too. The unmistakable odor of road-kill. Kat coughed and clasped her hand to her nose.

"Over there." Roger pointed to the tool bench at the back of the shadowy garage. They started toward it, carefully crossing around the deep rectangular repair bay pit in the floor. The floor was slippery with grease.

"Watch your step," Roger warned Kat as he pushed through the dangling hoist chains that suspended a massive truck engine high overhead.

They reached the tool bench, and Roger grabbed a small hammer. Not big enough. He squinted in the darkness, felt around on the bench, and found a screwdriver. He tested the tip, then felt down the front of the bench and pulled open the drawer.

A low, sliding sound came from the shadows at the far end of the bench. Roger spun around. Something was on the ground moving toward him. Roger brandished the screwdriver.

"What is it?" Kat whispered, alarmed; she looked

in the direction Roger was looking. But there was nothing there. "Roger?"

But Roger saw it all. A young girl emerged from the darkness. Her tank top was shredded by knife wounds; she clutched her severed legs in her hands as she dragged her torso along the garage floor, leaving a trail of blood.

Her desperate eyes met Roger's. "He...he's coming," she pleaded.

A loud metallic clang came from the corner opposite her. Roger looked over and saw another woman; some of her hair had been ripped from her scalp. An oily crankshaft jutted out from her chest, and it banged against the concrete floor as she crawled desperately toward him.

"Get it out. Please. Get it out of me," the impaled woman begged.

A third voice from beyond the air compressor caused Roger to spin again. This time he saw a blonde teenager with drill bits sunk deep into her eyes. She groped her way toward Roger as blood and bile oozed from the intestines that spilled from a deep gash in her bare torso. "I can't see anything. Help me...please."

Roger staggered back against the tool bench and closed his eyes tightly, trying to will away the horrific sights and sounds.

"Roger! Roger!" Kat grabbed him and pulled him around.

He opened his eyes and was met by Kat's terrified face. He looked back at the shadows. The spirits were gone.

Roger took a deep breath and tried to slow his racing heart "We're close...close to where he killed them."

Roger knew there was no other explanation.

There were too many of them, and the encounter had been too intense. Roger leaned back against the tool bench.

Kat rested her hand on his arm, concerned. "Are you going to be okay?" she asked.

Roger exhaled shakily, closed his eyes again.

"Roger, you've got to stay with me."

"I will. I'm trying."

He didn't have a choice. He had to be okay.

Roger had experienced "hot" zones before, but never like this. Usually it was at an intersection where there had been a violent car accident, and once it had even been in a 7-11.

It had been several years ago, after a late-night gig, and he was exhausted. His guard was down, and when he was coming back from the cold case with a six-pack, he saw a smear of blood across the aisle. Seconds later he was surrounded by two small children. One had been shot in the head and the other in the chest. Their mother had the side of her face blown off. Roger learned later that the family had been caught in the cross fire from a robbery that had gone horribly wrong.

As horrific as that encounter had been, this was far more intense. He was seeing Kincaid's victims in the moments of their death, and they had all died from some horrible kind of torture.

Roger opened his eyes again and turned back to the bench. He felt around inside the dark drawer and came up with a heavy pipe wrench. "Here," he said to Kat.

"Shhhh."

Roger turned in time to see Kincaid's silhouette in the entrance to the garage.

Kat was already frozen, staring at the ominous sight. She gently pulled Roger back into the shadows and looked around. "There's got to be another way out," she said.

There was. The back door that Kincaid had come through earlier to get his shotgun. She turned back to Roger and whispered, "Come on."

Kat steadied Roger as they crept over to the door and tried it. But it was now locked.

"Shit."

Roger looked back at the garage entrance. Kincaid stepped inside, carefully scanning the darkness. There was an icy, determined expression on his face as he started forward, shotgun at the ready. Like a focused animal that knew it had cornered its prey. There was no way they could get past him and out that front door without him seeing them.

Kat tugged on Roger's arm again. He looked back. She was pointing at one of the small storage room doors off in the corner. It would have to do.

They hurried over. Kat quietly tried the knob, and it opened.

Across the garage, Kincaid swept the barrel of the shotgun through the dangling engine-hoist chains, pushing them out of his way. He crept along the edge of the repair pit, keeping his eyes and ears carefully attuned to the darkness around him.

It was nearly black inside the small, narrow storage room when Roger quietly closed the door behind them. The only source of pale light came from a small, dirty window on the far side that had been papered over with yellowing newspaper. The acrid smell of road-kill was intense; Kat gagged and stifled a cough.

"The window," Roger said as he felt his way across the narrow room.

Kat followed behind him, holding her hands

outstretched in front of her. She was almost to the other side when her right hand brushed against something. She hesitated, lowered her hand, and felt the edge of a workbench. Feeling more certain now, she slid her hand along the edge of the bench, using it to guide her way. After several steps, her fingers hit something and she paused.

It was cold, wet and clay-like.

She squinted down into the pitch-blackness, trying to see. "Roger! Roger, something's in here."

Roger found his way to the small window. He reached up high, stretching as far as he could and managed to get a loose corner of the yellowing newspaper that covered it. He gave a yank, tearing away the dirt-covered windowpane.

Pale light streamed in, revealing the room for the first time.

They were in the middle of Kincaid's "art gallery."

It was a charnel house filled with strange sculptures made from human fingers, arms, toes, and teeth, welded together with engine parts. All of them were macabre, grisly fusions of man and machine. Roger remembered the sculpture he had seen Kincaid working on in the garage. Had someone's body parts been destined to be part of that one, also?

Kat stumbled back, horrified, and in the process slammed into Kincaid's current project, Lucinda. Her freshly dismantled body was strewn out on the workbench.

Kat opened her mouth to scream, but Roger slapped his hand over her mouth and pointed.

The shadow of Kincaid's feet appeared on the other side of the crack at the bottom of the door.

Roger and Kat remained frozen as Kincaid's

shadow moved up to the door and paused. Kat's terrified eyes were torn between the shadow under the door and the macabre gallery around her. What kind of thoughts ran through a mind like Kincaid's? She struggled to find logic to his endeavors. A mechanic, yes. A man who worked with machines and engines. But the grafting of human flesh with cold steel?

Kat could understand the creative mind. The music she immersed herself in was often dark and disturbing. But music was art. A metaphor for some kind of emotion or experience, sometimes purely designed to elicit a reaction, which was in and of itself a valid reason to exist. But this was abomination around her. Was it the ultimate freedom of expression for Kincaid? The creative mind that dared to create with impunity? To will an abstract into reality, no matter what the cost? Or was it something born of a disconnect between what was living and what was machine? An inability to distinguish the machines he made come alive from the living people he used to do so? The corporal, mechanical and functional human body equating itself intimately with man-made machines. How could you leap to such a thought? And disturbingly enough, what a free artist Kincaid truly must be to avoid any censorship, no matter what the cost.

Kat's mind raced as her eyes took in the creations all around her. She was thinking about this too rationally. There couldn't be a reason any sane, thinking mind could ascribe to it. His disconnect with reality had to be so far afield that she could never begin to comprehend. No. It was madness. Not art. It was not understandable. It was mutilation and insanity.

The time Kat and Roger remained frozen felt like an eternity. But, in fact, it had been only seconds. Kat's thoughts had raced so quickly, she had lost track.

Roger had moved up to the edge of the door, and he was now holding the wrench up high, waiting to make a desperate attempt at clubbing Kincaid if he came through that door.

Then, as if the monster instinctively knew there was a threat awaiting him, the shadow on the other side of the door crack moved away. They heard his footsteps retreat back into the garage.

Roger lowered the wrench. "Let's get out of here," he whispered as he pushed past Kat, who remained frozen and near shock.

He squinted down into the darkness below the window and could barely make out a toolbox. He carefully placed his foot on it, tested it, and then stepped up onto it. He quietly opened the latch at the bottom of the window frame and pushed outward. Thunk! The frame hit something.

Roger wiped away the heavy film of dirt on the glass and revealed the reason: There were metal bars on the outside of the window.

"Shit," Roger whispered. They were stuck. No way out.

Twenty One

Kat sank to her knees in the corner, trembling, tears welling in her eyes. "We're dead. We're dead," she whispered shakily.

Roger turned and saw the broken and vulnerable woman as she wrapped her arms around her legs and pulled them close to herself. He felt everything she was feeling; there wasn't a way out of this that he could see, but he knew it wouldn't do anyone any good to give up.

He crossed over, kneeled down next to her. "No, it's not over yet. We'll get out."

They sat a moment in silence, and Kat rested her head on his shoulder. Roger felt her against him, and he reached out and put his arm around her.

Kat took a trembling breath as tears spilled over and ran down her cheeks. "Where the fuck are we going to go? He knows we didn't leave. It's only a matter of time before he comes back here. He'll find us. He's going to kill us."

Roger looked down at the heavy wrench in his hand. "Not without a fight."

"Against a shotgun? He's got a fucking shotgun."

Roger didn't have an answer to that. He pulled her a little closer, and they settled into silence again.

Kat wiped her eyes, took a deep breath, and stared off into the darkness, avoiding the grisly sculptures that filled the room. How had she gotten here? She tried to trace everything that had happened, looking for the answer, and trying to find someone to blame. But there was no one. She had been working all this time with this hell all around her. Roger had only discovered it. In the end, Kincaid would have probably come for her the way he had for her mother.

Her mother.

The guilt Kat felt for being so angry at her mother for leaving again, when, in fact, she had been so brutally murdered, ate away at Kat; it was worse than knowing she now faced certain death.

Kat spoke softly, breaking the silence. "Did you see her? Did you see my mother when you went over?"

Roger looked down at her searching, desperate eyes. He could tell she needed something to hold onto right now. And he was willing to do anything he could to ease her pain. So he lied.

"Yeah. I did."

A sad smile appeared on Kat's tear-streaked face and Roger could see that his lie was a comfort to her "She wanted to tell you that she was sorry," he continued. "She wanted you to know she didn't just leave you again. She wanted you to know she…" Roger paused, swallowed dryly, and added, "She wanted you to know she loved you very much."

Kat closed her eyes, letting his words touch her deeply. "I always knew it. I mean I just…I don't know, I just felt it. Even after she left the second time, somehow I knew there had to be a reason."

Roger looked down at the fragile woman in his arms and knew he had said the right thing. But he also knew she wasn't lying to herself. She probably had felt those things from her mother; it was entirely possible that her mother had reached out to her from the other side.

Roger had met several other sensitives in his life, some stronger than others, but he also realized that most people had the ability to feel things from the other side if they allowed themselves.

They sat for another moment without saying anything. But the very reason they could sit there in the darkness as the minutes ticked by was starting to make Roger restless. Was this going to be how it ended for them? Were they going to sit here until Kincaid came back and found them? There had to be a way they both wouldn't die.

Roger's thoughts started to magnify themselves along with a newfound anger. He found himself shaking his head. "I'm not going to do this," he said.

Kat looked over at him, not understanding.

Roger felt his resolve solidifying. "I'm not going to sit here and wait for him." He pulled away from Kat. "One way or another, I'm going out there." He got to his feet and looked back down at her. "Stay here. If you hear something, run. I'll do what I can to distract him."

Kat wiped her eyes as she looked up at Roger. She knew what he was suggesting; he was willing to sacrifice himself so that she could escape. But there was no way she was going to let him.

"No," she said firmly. "I don't want to stay here alone."

She meant it. She would rather die trying to escape with him than have him leave her alone to fend for herself.

But Roger pushed his point. "Kat, as long as he's busy with me, you might have a chance."

"I don't care. I don't want to be here alone. I'm going with you."

Roger looked down at her and saw the determination on her frightened face; he knew he wouldn't be able to change her mind. And he was right.

* * *

Moments later, the storeroom door opened a crack. Roger carefully peered out. The garage was silent. There was no sign of Kincaid.

Roger opened the door a little further and stepped out, brandishing the heavy wrench. He looked back at Kat and signaled. She came out behind him.

"I don't see him," Roger whispered.

They both scanned the dark maze of shadows between them and the open front door. A glimmer of hope. Maybe they would be okay after all.

"Let's get out before he comes back," Kat whispered urgently, and nudged Roger.

They started tentatively toward the open door across the large garage. They reached the repair bay and carefully crept around the side to the dangling engine-hoist chains. Roger looked back at Kat and pointed out the chains so that she would be careful not to disturb them. Kat nodded silently, and Roger squeezed carefully around them.

Kat started to follow him, and her foot slipped on the oily floor. She recoiled to catch her balance, and her arm brushed against the chains. They rattled as they swayed back and forth.

They both froze in their tracks.

Roger frantically searched the shadows around them. The garage remained quiet. No sign of Kincaid.

Another lucky break. They pressed onward. The open door was straight in front of them now, about ten yards away. They picked up their pace. Seven yards to go… then six… five… four… then it was just a few steps, and they were there. Roger paused and carefully peered outside.

The dark truck stop was quiet. There was no sign of anyone. Roger adjusted his angle so that he could see around the side of the main building to the parking lot.

They had a clear path all the way to his car at the front of the diner.

Roger allowed himself to feel a glimmer of hope. They were close now. The end was in sight.

He turned back to Kat, and that was when the shadows came alive behind her. Kincaid stepped out and leveled his shotgun at them.

Roger tackled Kat. BOOM! The shotgun blasted over their heads.

They tumbled back into the garage. Kincaid racked his gun again and cut in front of the open door, blocking their escape.

"Kat! Up! Get up!" Roger yelled as he dragged Kat to her feet. They frantically stumbled back deeper into the garage.

Kincaid started after them, his shotgun leveled and ready. Roger and Kat pushed their way through the dangling hoist chains.

Kincaid took aim at Roger. It was close range, no way he could miss. Roger desperately hurled the heavy wrench at Kincaid. It glanced off his shoulder—BOOM! It was a wild shot.

Roger backed into the chains, looking frantically all around for any possible way out of this. Kincaid racked the shotgun again, bearing down on Roger. His finger moved to the trigger. Finally. The last, fatal shot.

In that split second, Roger saw a way out. He reached up, yanked the lock lever on the hoist chain, and it sprung free. The massive truck engine suspended above plunged downward.

Kincaid leaped back, but not far enough to get out of the way of the heavy engine as it rattled downward. The massive motor crashed down on Kincaid's leg, pinning him to the greasy floor. The shotgun clattered into the bottom of the repair pit.

Twenty Two

The loud noise echoed into silence. Roger and Kat took a moment to assess their new situation. Kincaid was trapped; the massive engine was lodged on his leg.

Roger reached down, retrieved the heavy wrench he had thrown at Kincaid, and staggered over to him.

"Where is she?" Roger said, catching his breath.

Kincaid grimaced in agony, blood pooled around his crushed leg. But Roger wasn't going to sit around and wait for an answer; this was his show now. Roger reared back and kicked Kincaid hard in the ribs.

Kincaid coughed and spit up blood. "Wh…who?" He growled in pain.

"You know who. My daughter. You took her from my car."

Kincaid shook his head "I…I didn't."

Roger kicked him hard again. "Don't fuck with me. You saw her in my car when I got here. You waited until I went into the diner. Where the fuck is she?"

A strange, twisted smile crossed Kincaid's bloody lips. He coughed, sputtered and started to laugh. "You…you're crazier…than I am."

Roger boiled over; he crushed his foot down onto Kincaid's shoulder. "Tell me!"

Kincaid grimaced in pain and gasped, "Okay, okay. Just get this…engine off my…leg."

"Not a fucking chance. Not until you tell me."

Kincaid's steely eyes shot a look up at Roger as he tried to catch his breath. "You…you really want to know?"

"Talk!"

Kincaid coughed, spit up more blood, and a

crooked smile twisted his thin lips. "I…cut off her head, and then I…I fucked her skull."

Kat gasped, horrified, and turned away. This was too much.

Kincaid continued, "Then I…I plowed through her little cunt with a…chainsaw."

Roger trembled with rage, overwhelmed by the vile monster.

Kincaid's eyes lit up, enjoying Roger's hell; his gasping laughter swelled. "Finally, I…I tore her little titties off with pliers and took a shit all over her."

Roger let out an enraged roar and slammed the heavy wrench down onto Kincaid's shoulder. The demon bellowed in agony.

"Liar! She's not dead! I know she's not dead! I didn't see her on the other side! I would have seen her!" Roger exploded.

Kincaid gasped for air, his breathing was ragged and shallow. He shook his head. "And…I told you I didn't…see her either. There was no one…in your…car when you got here."

Roger glared down at the monster, and a dark determination overwhelmed him. "You want to play it this way? I can play it this way. I'll do this all night until you…."

Then he heard it. A faint voice calling out from the distance. "Daddy! Daddy?"

Roger froze instantly. He stopped breathing. His heart stopped. He heard it again. A faint, small, far-away little voice. "Daddy! Where are you?"

Roger looked toward the open garage door. It was her.

"Lilly!" He dropped the wrench, looked over at Kat. "It's her. It's Lilly." He bolted away.

"Roger! Wait!" Kat yelled after him, but he was

already out the door.

* * *

Roger raced outside the garage and paused. He scanned the dark junkyard in the distance. "Lilly!"

"Daddy!" her little voice called back. Roger locked on the direction. It was coming from the parking lot in front.

"Lilly, where are you?"

"I'm here, Daddy. I'm here!"

Roger took off up the side of the truck stop and cut into the parking lot. He paused, catching his breath. There was no sign of her. "Honey! Where are you?"

"Daddy!" she called back. Then he zeroed in on the direction. It was coming from inside his car.

Roger raced over, splashing through the mud puddles. "Oh God, Lilly." He peered in the wet window on the passenger side.

Lilly was right there, under the blanket in back, her pink rabbit in her arms.

A flood of relief and joy overwhelmed Roger. He trembled ecstatically as he tried the door handle, but it was locked. "Open the door, honey. It's me. I'm right here."

"I can't, Daddy, I can't." Lilly's muffled little voice replied.

Roger frantically searched his pockets and dug out his keys "It's okay, it's all right. Hold on. Just hold on."

He flipped through the ring for his car key; his shaking fingers fumbled them. They splashed into the mud puddle below the door. "Shit!" he cursed.

Roger dropped to his knees and started frantically feeling for the keys under the murky water.

Kat appeared around the corner of the truck stop, out of breath. She saw him searching the mud puddle. "Roger?" she called out, puzzled.

Roger looked up at her, smiling. "She's here! She's in my car!"

Kat started toward Roger; this was all happening so fast it was hard for Kat to figure out what was going on. "What? What did you say?"

"She found her way back. Somehow she found her way back," Roger explained.

Kat reached the car as Roger found his keys under the water. He yanked them out. "Got 'em!"

Roger looked up at Kat triumphantly. Then everything went horribly wrong.

Kincaid was hobbling on a bleeding leg into the parking lot behind Kat; his shotgun was aimed and ready.

"NO!" Roger leaped up and shoved Kat out of the way just as….

BOOM!

The slug meant for Kat slammed into Roger's chest. He plunged to the wet pavement.

"Roger!" Kat yelled, horrified.

Kincaid racked his shotgun, took aim at Kat.

BOOM BOOM BOOM! New gunfire erupted from somewhere else in the parking lot. The bullets pelted Kincaid. He crumpled to the ground, revealing two newly arrived policemen behind him. They moved in, covering him.

Kat crawled over to Roger. She reached down and cradled his head in her hands. Blood oozed from his chest. "Roger," she said. "Roger, can you hear me?"

Roger looked up at her desperately. "She… she's in the back seat. She's there. Help her." He weakly raised his hand, holding the keys.

Kat took them and hesitated.

"Get her out of there," he insisted.

Kat lowered Roger's head back to the ground. She pulled herself to her feet and turned to the car. She carefully slipped the key in the lock, gave it a turn and pulled open the door.

The back seat was empty except for a rumpled blanket.

Lilly wasn't there.

Kat searched the front seat. Nothing. No sign of the little girl.

Kat turned back, kneeled at Roger's side. "Roger? Roger, what did you see? There's no one there. There's no one in the car."

Dear God, no. Roger felt a bleak darkness begin to swallow him up. Of all the times he had been cruelly tortured by his visions, this was the cruelest.

"Roger?" Kat could see Roger's expression become distant and lost, and he didn't answer her.

One of the policemen who had just arrived ran up, barking into his radio. "I need emergency services. Stat! I've got a gunshot wound to the chest." He clicked off. "Ma'am. Are you all right?" he asked Kat.

Kat could only nod vaguely as she held Roger.

"This is Dalton, isn't it? Roger Dalton?"

Kat nodded again "Yeah."

The policeman pulled out a satellite phone and punched a number.

* * *

Zoe's street in the aging tract home development in Las Vegas was lit up with the flickering lights from the emergency vehicles. There were several police cars, a forensics truck, an ambulance, and a morgue van.

Uniformed police and detectives swarmed the walkway up to Zoe's condo.

The evidence from the firefight inside the condo was everywhere. Bullet holes in the walls, shattered lamps and tables.

A homicide detective in his early 60s was on his satellite phone, talking to the policeman at Cedar Mountain Truck Stop. "Dalton? Are you sure? This is one weird fucking night. All right, it's gonna take a while to sort all of this out. Anything changes, let me know."

He punched off the phone and looked down at the bullet-riddled body of Roger's ex-wife, Zoe. Next to her was Jack, her drug-dealing boyfriend.

But this wasn't a fresh crime scene.

Both bodies were starting to smell and decay; they were pale, and the dark blood had pooled on the bottom of their torsos, arms and legs.

Another detective approached. "The condo next door is vacant," he said to his colleague. "No one heard the shots. If we hadn't come looking for the daughter, who knows how long before this would've been found."

The detective looked down at Zoe's boyfriend. "Jack Murphy, that piece of shit. Let's hope this puts an end to the fucking drug war he started."

The detective wasn't surprised that he had found Jack this way—he knew it would happen some day. Jack had pissed off a lot of low level mobsters in Las Vegas.

A uniformed policeman called from the hallway. "Detective! We've got something else in here."

The detective crossed to the hallway and approached an officer who was standing at an open bedroom door; the officer was pale and shaken.

"Oh, Jesus." The detective stopped cold, choking back a reaction. He'd seen a lot through his years on the force, but things like this never got easier.

Lilly's body was under the bloodstained bed covers.

The detective looked away, sickened. "Get forensics in here."

The policeman nodded and started away. The detective hesitated a moment, then looked back into the room. The details. It was always the details of things like this that made it so hard. He could see Lilly's little hand still clutching her favorite stuffed animal, its pink fur soaked with dried blood. The detective had bought one just like it for his granddaughter.

It was a popular toy, and it looked similar to the muddy remains that Roger had found in the junkyard; it was understandable how he had been mistaken.

The detective looked away again; he would read the forensics report and learn more than he ever wanted to learn about this little girl's last moments on earth.

But he still wouldn't know everything. He'd never know that two nights ago Lilly had waited for her daddy to come. She never got his message that he was going to be a couple of days late; her mother was too strung out to remember to tell her. Lilly had told Jimmie Jerry that her daddy was coming, and he would take her away from all this soon. It hadn't been soon enough.

Lilly had just kissed Jimmie Jerry goodnight when she heard the arguing and the gunshots in the living room. She called out for her mother, but there was no answer. Before she could get out of bed, the man appeared in her doorway.

The last thing Lilly saw was the flash from the

pistol barrel that took her life-.

The night *before* Roger arrived to pick her up.

* * *

The sky at the Cedar Mountain Truck Stop was beginning to glow with a dull grey light. It wouldn't be long now before the sun rose.

"Roger. Roger, stay with us," Kat pleaded as she held Roger's hand; there were tears in her eyes as the policeman frantically did compressions on his chest and listened for any signs that he would resume breathing.

"Come on. Come on, breathe for me!" The policeman gasped.

Kat clung to Roger's limp hand. "Roger! Roger, please."

The policeman paused, put his ear to Roger's lips and heard a long, slow exhale. He did several more pumps, then turned to Kat, exhausted. "It's no use, he's…I'm sorry."

Kat placed Roger's hand on his chest. She reached up and gently brushed the hair from his eyes, and that's when she noticed that there was a warm smile on Roger's lifeless face. He was somewhere else now, seeing something else…

He was seeing Lilly.

* * *

The dead-world had never looked so beautiful to Roger. The sun was breaking over the mountains surrounding the truck stop as he kneeled in front of his daughter with his arms outstretched.

The little girl ran to him and he held her tight. "I'm sorry, honey. I'm so sorry. I won't leave you with your mommy again, I promise. I know it's not safe there."

Lilly clung to her father, and there was wisdom in her eyes far beyond her years as she whispered into his ear, "It's okay, Daddy. I came with you. I've been with you the whole time. I'll never let you go."

Tears brimmed in Roger's eyes. He was home now in her arms, right where he knew he was always meant to be.

THE END